Duplicity

- A Novel

KATRINA AVANT

Katrina'sWORKS
PUBLISHING

ISBN-13: 978-0692380437
ISBN-10: 0692380434

Duplicity
Copyright © February 2015
Katrina Avant
K a t r i n a a v a n t - a u t h o r . c o m

Editor
L.R. Clark

Cover Design
Katrina'sWORKS
K a t r i n a s w o r k s . c o m

Dedication

Duplicity is dedicated to those who saw the dream of Katrina'sWORKS and believed. It is through your prayers and support that I am able to continue my dream, as well as the dreams of others who have the desire to become published authors. I greatly appreciate YOU!

Thank You!

Prologue

Teddy Reid ground his teeth as he pounded down the lid on the fifty-five gallon drum. Once again he was cleaning up someone else's mess. This time it was for Riley's sister. Reese had called him from the warehouse near hysterics. He couldn't make out what she was saying, but understood why once he arrived. She had killed Carrington Hayes.

Brushing a grimy sleeve across his sweaty brow, he stopped his work to glance over at Reese. She stood just a few feet away; fingering the charms on the bracelet he had given her for her birthday. When he arrived, he found her in the same spot; hovering over Hayes' body with a bloody hammer clutched to her chest. She had used it to bludgeon him to death. Teddy grimaced. Knowing Hayes' arrogant playboy antics, he didn't have to ask what happened. More than likely she had confronted him on his cheating.

Teddy blinked. All of this could have been avoided if she could have just given him a chance and accepted him for the man she needed. He wanted to be more than her friend, but she saw him as just another one of her brother's flunkies, and not someone to be taken seriously. Even with her standing there covered in blood, he loved her and would do anything for her. Maybe now she would look at him as a man, he thought. She did call him to help her. She had to feel something for him.

Irritated, Teddy raked his teeth over his bottom lip. He knew Hayes would be trouble the moment he started sniffing around her. The guy was no good and he told Reese so. But even though the man was an ass, he thought the most that could happen, would be Reese crying over a broken heart, not him concealing a body. Clearing his throat, Teddy turned back to his work. He wished Reese had taken his advice and left the fool alone.

Finished with his task, he pinched the bridge of his nose. Now he had to find a place to put the damn thing where it could never be found. But first he needed to get Reese to snap out of it. She had been standing in the same spot since he arrived. She just stood there in a daze; in shock at what she'd done. She was so out of it, he had to pry the hammer from her hand before wiping it down and tossing it in with the body.

"I…I don't know what happened. One minute we were arguing and the next thing I knew he was laying on the floor." Reese knelt down to touch the spot Teddy had scrubbed cleaned.

He grabbed her up by her shoulders. "Reese, listen to me. You have to get out of here before someone shows up. Reese…" Teddy shook her; shook her hard. She had to snap out of it. Although they were in a part of the building that was rarely used, they could still be discovered if one of the crew decided to wander in, looking for some alone time with one of the girls. They were in a secluded warehouse owned and operated by the mayor.

Realizing she wasn't going to move, Teddy decided to forego his plans to bury the drum. He couldn't do that and take care of Reese too. He would have to improvise. Acting quickly, he pulled her to his car and placed her in the passenger seat. Finding a screwdriver, he punched several holes in the top of the drum. He would have to toss the barrel into the river. With any luck, it would sink to the bottom, never to be seen again.

Duplicity

Chapter 1

Kobe stared unseeingly at the breaking news ticker that ran across the bottom of the muted television screen mounted behind the bar. Councilman Hayes' son was missing. The headliner only vaguely registered, because his mind was where it always was; on Bria.

The death of Bria Talbert still haunted him. He blamed himself. If he hadn't suggested she come to Jamaica, she would still be alive. And on top of that, he never got a chance to tell her that he loved her. He had wasted five good years not pursuing his attraction, and when he finally had the chance to make love to her, in a matter of hours she was dead. This was all due to his carelessness. He should have been there to shield her from those bullets, but instead, they had run in opposite directions to take cover from Grey's surprise attack. If he had just stuck by her side...

Private investigator Kobe West was good at his job; at least he thought he had been. Until that fatal day in

Jamaica, when his long time colleague and newly
christened girlfriend Bria Talbert was killed, he considered
himself one of the best. Up until that moment, his record
was flawless. Kobe was meticulous and always careful; no
one died on his watch. For the most part, working for a law
firm didn't bring that level of violence into his life; not
until Jamaica. He blamed himself for Bria's death, because
he'd become lax; never expecting what happened, but felt
he should have. He knew Grey was a predator, so he should
have prepared accordingly. His slackness had cost Bria her
life.

Mentally brushing away the constant agony, Kobe
glanced over his shoulder at the players in his latest
assignment. The four men were sitting at a nearby table,
boozing it up. They must have had a productive day,
because they were annoying the bar patrons with their
obnoxious and boisterous behavior.

Sighing, he rubbed his eyes; wondering if he would
be able to get a good night's sleep once this assignment
ended. It had been a year since Bria, and he still hadn't
gotten a decent night's rest. Apart from the restless nights,
whenever he did find himself drifting off, she haunted his
dreams. He often woke reaching out for her, and then later

mourning from the realization that she was gone, never to return. He hoped for sleep soon; no dreams just sleep.

This latest assignment involved working a joint case with one of Tor Hudson's investigators. The collaboration was suggested by his boss and good friend, Matthias Bennett. Matthias felt Kobe needed some time away from the office—and memories of Bria. Kobe glanced back once more at the rowdy crew. The group had grown louder to everyone's dismay. The other customers kept glaring at them; hoping they would catch the hint and quiet down or leave.

Dressed in ill-fitting business suits, the group of would be business men were oblivious to the others in the establishment. They were too busy knocking back shots and rehashing old street stories to care what the others thought. Kobe considered them could be business men, because they had no actual office to report to. This group's duties were to lurk around dark alleys and other low places instead of brokering deals in boardrooms of corporate America.

Despite their attire, Kobe knew the foursome were thinly disguised muscle for a couple of politicians suspected of voter fraud. With the important state and citywide elections fast approaching, the state's attorney general wanted to make sure none of the candidates gained an upper hand illegally. The current mayor was suspected of using a little persuasion to win his last election, and it was rumored that this time would be no different. Not knowing how far the mayor's reach extended within the police department, the AG hired the outside agency to counteract detection.

Kobe checked his watch; it was still early. He had a couple more hours to hang before he could call it a night. He had hoped the men would let something slip or meet with a common link between the mayor's office and a suspected city councilman. They needed just one connection to further their investigation.

He checked his watch again and frowned. Although he was supposedly working this assignment with one of Tor's investigators, he had yet to meet the guy. He was told he was working another angle, but would meet up with him tonight to compare notes. Kobe wondered what was keeping him; he expected the man an hour ago.

***

KT Ellis peered through the window at Kobe hunched over a beer at the far end of the bar. She knew she was late, thanks to Eric Valero, her police detective boyfriend. She should have known stopping by his place for a quick visit was a bad idea. A quick stop at his home always resulted in her staying longer than planned. But she had been working long hours and hadn't had time to see him. She missed him and obviously he missed her by the way he greeted her. KT smiled when she remembered how well Eric greeted her.

Bringing her thoughts back to the present, she searched the crowd for their targets. She didn't have to search long before hearing the bunch laughing loudly at something that was said. She shook her head. If they were supposed to be keeping a low profile, they were doing a very poor job of it. She silently roasted the sloppiness and unprofessionalism of the crew of street cops. They either didn't know how to be discreet or just arrogant enough not to care. KT shook her head again. She knew their carelessness would be their down fall.

Having kept Kobe waiting long enough, she pushed open the door.

***

Lifting his glass to his lips, Kobe grimaced when the men managed to become even more rowdy; punctuating this latest uproar with whistles and cat calls. He craned his neck to see what brought on this level of commotion. It didn't take him long to spot the source for the outburst. A woman had entered the bar. Kobe's mouth tightened as he swallowed the cool liquid from his glass. With the way the men were eying her, there could be trouble.

With mild interest, he turned slightly to consider the lone woman, as she settled herself at the end of the bar. He casually noticed she had the right curves in the right places. He continued to assess her as she raised an elegant hand to capture the bartender's attention. She was attractive; slim; but not overly skinny like he felt most women were these days. He took in her pixie haircut which complimented her delicate features and high cheekbones. After observing her hair, he caught sight of expressive eyes framed by thick black lashes that were clearly not hers, but complimented her just the same. Lowering his gaze, he lingered briefly on full pouty lips that appeared barely tinted with a muted lip color.

Coming to his senses, Kobe mentally shook himself. She was a looker, but not for him. Aside from being raw from loosing Bria, he liked his women with a little toughness; the kind of toughness that made her a good investigator; the kind of toughness that should have kept her alive. Turning back to his drink, he was about to raise his hand for a second round when one of the obnoxious four's voice suddenly quieted the establishment. He was pissed. While Kobe was giving the newcomer the once over, the man had materialized in the woman's space.

"What the hell you mean no thank you? I just wanted to show you some hospitality that's all. You act like I invited you face first to my crotch or something." Talking loudly, the man glanced around the bar for support. The only support he gained was from his friends, who loudly urged him on. "You know, that's what's wrong with you stuck-up bitches. A man can't buy you a drink or pay you a compliment without you getting all snotty and defensive."

Not rising to the fight, KT ignored him. The inebriated man had offered her a drink to which she promptly declined.

Kobe's eyes narrowed as he watched the encounter. From the set of the man's jaw, he could tell he wasn't about to let it go.

Sucking his teeth in disgust, the man refused to leave. He wanted her to properly apologize after loudly calling her out on her rejection. But to his infuriation, KT responded by pulling her phone from her purse to place a call. He had been dismissed. This move angered the indignant man even more. Without warning, he waited until she placed the phone to her ear before grabbing hold of her wrist.

Kobe frowned. He would have to intervene and come to the woman's aide. Rising from his seat, he heard his phone buzz on the bar top. Ignoring the call, he placed the still ringing phone into his pocket. But before he could maneuver his way through the crowd, the woman swiftly took hold of the man's hand, and using his weight against him, flipped him onto his back without leaving her chair. The bar's patrons clapped and cheered their approval.

The bully went down cursing. He was livid; not so much because she had gotten the best of him in a crowded bar, but because his buddies were killing themselves laughing. They had goaded him into approaching the woman, only to have her take him down. Seething and embarrassed, he picked himself up from the floor to join his friends back at their table. He only glanced back once; cursing under his breath with every step.

With a slight grin, Kobe stopped to admire the woman's handy work. Clearly she didn't need his help or anyone else's in handling the situation. Curious, he decided to approach her anyway. He had to meet her. As he worked his way to her side, he heard someone snicker. The man bet his companion that he would be the next one to meet the floor. Kobe dismissed this. Unlike his predecessor, he knew how to approach a lady.

"Are you alright?" he asked, as he slid onto the stool next to her. She was taking a celebratory sip from her drink place. She nodded at the grinning bartender, before turning towards Kobe.

With a lick of her lips, KT set her glass down. "I am now. Why didn't you answer your phone?" she asked him; amused by the puzzled look on his face. She knew she wasn't what he expected the moment she entered the bar. Like the other patrons, he'd given her an audience, but unlike the others, he barely glanced at her. Kobe had immediately dismissed her as his contact.

Although she was use to getting attention whenever she rode her bike, she had detoured from her usual attire of biker gear or jeans. Tonight she dressed the part of an available woman to grab optimal attention. Her hope was to cozy up to one of the men to obtain information. But with the bully's reaction, and her need to put him in his place, put a stop to that plan. KT Ellis was about as tough as they came, but she could be as feminine as the next woman when the occasion arose. Rarely did she don dresses. In her line of work, there was little opportunity or need for such attire. But when times like these called for her to acclimate, she could pull it off with the killer style of a fashionista.

Kobe's brow furrowed; clearly puzzled. "I'm sorry…?" He had no idea what she was taking about. How could she have known his phone rang? She was too busy flooring that fool to notice him. Besides, she never even glanced in his direction.

KT resisted the urge to roll her eyes. It was always the same. Given their profession, along with her name, they always expected a man. "I'm the one who called you…you were supposed to meet me here…KT Ellis. Ring a bell now?" She gave him a full smile when it finally hit him. She was the investigator he was meeting.

Kobe blinked. He was shocked to say the least. It never occurred to him that KT Ellis was a woman. He'd sat at that bar over an hour expecting a man. He wondered if Matthias knew he would be working with a woman, and if so, why didn't he tell him? Kobe's jaw tightened on this. After Bria's death, he had no desire to work with another woman and Matthias knew it. Because he felt responsible for Bria's death, if something happened to another female under his watch, he didn't think he could handle it.

KT studied the emotions playing across Kobe's face. She could tell he was debating whether or not to continue with this job. Making a decision, she would let him off the hook. "Look, I know I'm probably not what you were expecting, so how about this. Why don't I have Tor assign you another investigator to work with…a male investigator?" Even though she could handle herself, she could understand his misgivings considering what happened in Jamaica. Tor had given her the rundown on Kobe and she could sympathize with him, even though it wasn't his fault.

He didn't want to ruffle any feathers, but Kobe agreed with her. He didn't think he could work with another female, not now anyway. They chatted a few minutes more, before KT paid for her drink and left. Taking his original seat, he sighed with relief. It was for the best. The assignment wasn't considered dangerous, but neither was the one in Jamaica. He didn't need another death on his conscience.

***

Riley Phillips watched KT cozy up to one of the guys who was sitting at the bar. His eyes narrowed when he witnessed the smile she gave him. Although his crew had moved on to the next topic of conversation and had ceased their ridicule of him, he was still smarting from the jabs they and the other patrons had given him over the incident.

Shifting his gaze from KT back to her companion, he sized him up. "Um…another pretty boy," he mumbled under his breath. He noticed Kobe when he first entered the bar earlier that evening. Phillips also noticed how the women's eyes lit up when the stranger swaggered to his seat, and this woman was no different.

Studying him closely, he realized he'd seen him there before tonight. He was always sitting alone nursing his drink; seeming to have the weight of the world on his shoulders. He figured whatever he was wrestling with must have been heavy, because he turned down all of the females who made a move on him. That didn't matter to Riley. What mattered was the fact he was able to cozy up to that spiteful bitch and he couldn't. He was sick of guys like him, always pulling the women. And the women always treating them, as if they were some sort of god; as if they deserved any and everything that they wanted. He wondered how confident Pretty Boy would be if he messed up that pretty face of his. Watch how he swaggers then, he thought.

Shifting back to KT, Riley sucked his teeth. If his boss hadn't pulled him and the guys from their normal duties, he would have run her in on assaulting a police officer. But his hands were tied. They couldn't draw any attention to themselves because of the election. He couldn't wait until the damn election was over. He was growing antsy. He needed to flex his muscles and so did his guys. But for now, they would play the role and roll with it—for now.

Taking one last longing look at the bitch at the bar, Riley grinned when she paid for her own drink and left. This gave him some satisfaction, but not much. She might not have allowed Pretty Boy to pay for her drink, but she still gave him attention. Phillips concluded; if they ever crossed paths again, he would make her pay; election or no election.

Chapter 2

Tor glanced up from the report he was reading to find KT standing in his doorway. Puzzled, he laid the report aside. She was supposed to be out with Kobe gathering information on the criminals they were investigating.

KT held up her hand. "Before you ask, everything is under control. At least I hope it will be." She said this last with uncertainty. While she was driving back to the office, she was beginning to rethink her offer to Kobe. She had never backed down from a case, no matter what the circumstances, and she questioned why she was doing so now. Sure Kobe was dealt a hard blow, but what did that have to do with her? She was good at her job and he should have been grateful Tor placed her with him.

Tor watched KT's wheels turn. He knew she was thinking long and hard about something and this piqued his interest. "So, are you going to tell me what's going on?"

"You know what…no. I got this. She made up her mind. Kobe West would have to lump it or leave it. Turning on her heels, she headed back to her car; and back to Kobe.

Tor shook his head and smiled. Knowing KT, if this was about Kobe not wanting to work with her, there will be hell to pay if he goes against her. And from what he was told by Matthias, he knew Kobe was probably the problem. Matthias had asked him to include him in their investigation to get his mind focused on something other than Bria's death. He agreed. He knew how hard it could be getting over the death of a friend. Tor had lost several during his tour with the Army, and it had to be doubly difficult to lose someone you loved.

Tor went back to his report with total confidence in KT. By the end of the conversation, she will make Kobe see things her way.

***

Kobe was still sitting at the bar when KT returned. Their rowdy suspects had called it a night. He was done for the day, but decided to stick around for a real drink, before heading home himself. He needed something stronger than the beer he'd been sipping on most of the evening.

"So I see the crew has scattered for the night. Did you get anything useful?" KT sat down next to him. Most of the bar's patrons had left.

Kobe eyed her through the bottom of his shot glass as he downed the amber liquid. "I didn't expect to see you again, especially not tonight," he commented; signaling the bartender for another round. "Can I get you a drink?"

"I'll have what he's having," KT told the woman serving Kobe. She returned the same fake smile the bartender had given her. She noticed the woman seemed put off by her arrival. Dropping the fake smile, the woman cut her eyes at KT before moving off to prepare their drinks. KT mentally shook her head. She guessed the woman had her own plans for Kobe. Any other time she would have conceded and helped the woman along, but this was business and they didn't need her hovering around.

Kobe shook his head to answer her question. "Nothing useful. Whatever they're up to, they're keeping it close. I may have to put in some extra surveillance time to see who they meet with in the morning. I did hear them say something about a package that's due to arrive right before the election; something to help make things go a little smoother." He held up his hands mimicking quotation marks. "I hope it's something to do with the proposed vote fixing. We need to catch a break on that end." He knocked back the scotch the bartender placed before him. To the woman's dismay, he accepted the drink and turned back to KT without acknowledging her. "Enough on that, what brings you back here?"

KT accepted her drink all the while noticing that the salty bartender was still eyeing her unrepentantly. She waited until the woman left to serve other customers, before answering him. "I've changed my mind; I'm not leaving this case." She watched as Kobe turned this over. She could tell he wasn't pleased to hear this; not pleased at all.

Kobe stared at her. He thought they had settled this, but decided to inquire on her change of heart before rebuking her. Granted, he didn't know the woman, but he still felt he shouldn't be working with her just the same. "Why not?"

"I understand you may have issues working with me as a woman, but I am damn good at my job and have been for many years. And not just as a civilian. Aside from my impeccable work as an investigator, I worked Special Ops alongside Tor during my stint in the Army, so there is no good reason for me to bow out of this assignment. So if you don't like it, *you* can take a walk, because I am here to stay." With that said she threw back her drink in one gulp.

He raised an interested eyebrow at her mention of Special Ops. Suddenly, Kobe saw KT with new eyes. Needing to say something, he opened his mouth then closed it again. He really couldn't argue with that point, seeing as he never served in any branch of the military, let alone Special Operations. He had a new respect for the lady. KT Ellis was much more than met the eye. And speaking of meeting the eye, this revelation seemed to have helped him to view her more clearly. He studied KT, as a man noticing an attractive woman for the first time, and not just casually.

Kobe admitted as before, she was an attractive woman. The white form fitting dress she wore followed every curve of her body, as if it were made just for her. He re-examined the taunt body he had dismissed too soon. Not only was KT fit, she was athletically fit. At first glimpse, he thought she was just another woman who chose private investigation for whatever reason. But because of her military credentials, it seemed the job chose her. Maybe he had judged her a little too quickly.

Resigned, Kobe shrugged. "Ok." This was all he gave her. What else could he say? The lady had more than made her point.

"Ok? Ok you're staying, or ok you're bowing out?"

"I'm staying. You've made your point." Truth be told, Kobe was impressed. He would have to do a little homework on Ms. KT Ellis to get the full picture of just who she was, but he was still impressed. When Matthias assigned him to this detail, he never asked who he would be working with. It never mattered as long as it wasn't with a woman. But after meeting KT, he wanted to know everything there was to know.

"Good." KT motioned for a different bartender. "I'm buying the next round."

***

Teresa "Reese" Phillips eyed the woman who sat laughing with Kobe with contempt. She thought she was done with that heffa for the night, when she left earlier. She had been trying to get Kobe to notice her all evening. Reese had set her sights on him when he first walked into the bar. He was the finest man she'd seen in a long time. When her coworker reached him before she did, she thought she had lost her chance; especially after he struck up a conversation with the woman who made her brother look like a fool. But after the crowd died down and the woman left, she made her move. In between serving customers, she made small talk with Kobe; angling for a chance to ask him out. But just before she could put her plan into play, that bitch comes back. She was the only woman in the whole place he showed any interest in and now she was back.

Reese knew she wasn't the most attractive woman in the world, but she had what her brother called presence. He said people like them may not be much to look at, but their presence always made people come around. But that old saying didn't always hold true; at least it didn't for him that night. Reese smirked. It had held true for her, at least for a little while. Her last boyfriend was known for all the model types he dated, but once she wowed him with her personality, among other things, he forgot all about those skinny skanks. It was too bad he stopped believing in her. They could have had a wonderful life together.

The thought of Carrington brought a deep frown to Reese's face. All Carrington had to do was love her and leave the others alone. When she asked him to meet her at the warehouse, she had all the proof she needed to confront him. The last time she tried to trip him up, he had her believing she was delusional with her accusations. But not this time. This time she had the photos and video to prove it.

She had suspected him long before she actually caught him. But once he forgot her birthday, she knew he had to be cheating; so she started tailing him. It didn't take long to obtain her proof. Carrington was back to his old tricks again; the tall skinny blondes. She was furious. When they met, he'd told her he'd found the love of his life—her. They were going to be married; settle down. He would start working for his fathers' company and she could leave her life of crime and become a loving housewife. But all that was gone now. The moment she confronted him, he laughed at her. Saying he could never marry someone as plain and unimportant as her; someone who came from the streets. He said Big Ed wouldn't have allowed it, even if he could get passed her dull plain Jane appearance. She was just a booty call; something to do until something better came along. The bastard had the nerve to insult her further by commenting on how good she was with her mouth.

That's when she picked up the hammer and started hitting him. She didn't know how many times it connected, only that when she finally stopped, he was lying on the floor with half a face and his torso caved in. Panicked, she had called Teddy. She knew he would know what to do. It seemed to have taken forever for her to place the call. The phone kept slipping through her bloody hands and it didn't help that she still held the hammer. By the time the call connected, she was shaking so bad, she couldn't remember enough to tell him what happened. Teddy told her not to speak to anyone and just stay there. She recalled nodding and dropping the phone, but not dropping her bloody weapon.

She was grateful to Teddy. He was the only real friend she ever had. Once he arrived, he never asked questions. He just took control and did what was needed to be done. After he got her home that night, he even bathed her and put her to bed. When she woke the next morning, she found him sitting in a chair next to her bed asleep. He had stayed with her the whole night.

Closing her eyes, Reese took a deep and calming breath. She hadn't allowed herself to think much on that night and there was no way she could talk about it. She and Teddy vowed to never speak of it again, not even to her brother Riley. And they hadn't. It was almost as if it never happened.

Reese's eyes narrowed at a melodic sound that jerked her out of her reverie. KT was laughing at something Kobe said. "I should have spit in her drink," she mumbled, just as her phone buzzed. Pulling her eyes from the couple, she retrieved the vibrating phone from her back pocket. Willing away the tenseness that had set in, Reese rolled her shoulders. She'd received the text she'd been waiting for. A new shipment had come in. She only hesitated a moment. She wanted to stay just in case KT left again. Shaking her head, she knew she couldn't. It wouldn't bode well for her if she was late taking care of business; not with that freak running the show. Taking one last longing look at Kobe, she grabbed her keys and left.

Chapter 3

The water barely rippled as the lifeless body was pushed beneath the surface of the dark, muddy water. The woman's matted and bloody hair clung to her torn face, even as her head bobbed against the waves. It only floated above the water a few seconds more, before it too disappeared into the deep. This was the fourth such body placed into the river by Metro City's unknown killer.

Agitated, the man leaned over the edge of the secluded pier to wash his blood-spattered hands in the now infamous Belle River. He hadn't wanted to kill her; not this one, and not this soon. But the urge had been too great. Rising from the wooden pier, he clenched his fists, as he drew in great gulps of the cool, damp air to calm himself. Never had he snatched a random woman off the street. He couldn't lose control like this again or he would surely be caught.

He always targeted his prey; getting to know them; their habits; their likes and dislikes. He would even interact with them days before he abducted them. Even asking one out on a date. Had she known what would happen on the end of that date, she would have ran from him screaming, instead of sizing him up as a potential mate. He laughed. She was desperate and lonely. Her biological clock ticking away. Well he took care of that for her. He almost hated to stab the hope from that one's eyes; eyes that looked at him with 'what could have been'.

Rocking on the balls of his feet, he took in another deep calming breath. He couldn't understand what went wrong this time. Why did the need to kill surge through his body without warning? This woman was nothing to him. He had never laid eyes on her before tonight. She just happened to be there in his space; in the wrong place at the wrong time. And if it hadn't been her, would he have chosen another? He liked to think that he wouldn't. He liked to think the moment would have passed had she not happened along.

Dismissing this for the moment, he grabbed up a beer from the six-pack he'd brought with him. He would get it right next time. He would stick to the plan. Twisting off the bottle cap, he downed the cool liquid in two gulps. Now that felt better. This was a part of the ritual he savored almost as much as the kill. There was nothing like a nice cold one after a brutal butchering. He marveled at how this one tried to be brave; tried not to cry. He had to admit, she was a tough one. But in the end, he stabbed and cut the toughness right out of her. No matter the reaction, they all submitted in the end.

The first woman he took pleaded for her life. She tried to appeal to him by bringing up her husband and children. It didn't work. Why should she get to live in a nice fairytale of a life, with an adoring family, when he couldn't have one? So when the second one started to cry and plead, he taped her mouth shut. He didn't want to hear her weak pathetic cries. It wasn't that her words touched him, not the way it would have a normal personal. He found her pleas to be too annoyingly normal. And he knew no matter how he tried, no matter what he did, he could never be normal. Sure he could blend in with the pack and become unrecognizable for what he really was, but he could never resist the urges that made him different, never.

When he was a child his father saw him for what he was and taught him to hunt. His good old dad thought this would purge that desire from his system; and it had worked—for awhile. His urges were soothed with the death of a deer or the rabbits they killed for food. His father said he shouldn't harm anything that he couldn't cook. This was their ritual. So all through his teens he would hunt until the urge passed. Then one day it was just gone. It was as if someone flipped a switch, allowing him to feel as if he could live a normal life. He thought it had disappeared and it had until a few months ago. And On its return, animals wouldn't do. Not this time. This time he needed more.

Chapter 4

"Twenty-nine year old Carrington Hayes has been missing since early yesterday morning…" The news commentator was saying.

City councilman Edward "Big Ed" Hayes stared intently at the breaking news story regarding his son. Running his fingers through his thinning hair, he found little satisfaction in viewing the first run story. He knew if he had been just another John Q. citizen, the police wouldn't have bothered to look for his Carrington, let alone the media giving the story any crucial airtime. But he wasn't just another man and his son wasn't just another citizen; Carrington was Big Ed's son and Big Ed demanded satisfaction.

Normally Big Ed wouldn't have thought anything of Carrington's absence, but when his Porsche Carrera GT was found abandoned in the rail yard, he began to think differently. Knowing his son's love for that car, he immediately feared Carrington had met with foul play and demanded police involvement in finding him.

Carrington Edward Hayes was Big Ed's only child; born and bred to be the best at whatever he chose to do. And what Carrington chose to do in his present life was to be a spoiled playboy. Ed always claimed that Carrington had time to come to grips with responsibility, but until he did, he showered him with whatever he wanted. Nothing was too good for him.

Big Ed was one of the city's more prominent councilmen. He started his political career around the same time mayor Craven Wallace began his. Unlike Wallace, Big Ed came from old money. His family made their fortune in imports. Back in the countries infancy, their main source of revenue came through the importing of slaves. Today the clan's money was made importing and exporting the most highly sought after goods for the elite of various societies around the world.

"In other news, Metro City PD has yet to find any clues from the latest body pulled from the river this afternoon. MCPD had hoped to find evidence linking the dead woman to the identity of the city's newly christened Belle River Killer. The woman…"

Big Ed frowned before switching off the flat screen. He turned to look out at his view of the river. Has his son become a victim of Metro City's killer? Big Ed shook his head, dismissing the idea. The bodies that were found had all been women. He didn't think the killer would shift gears and start killing men. Would he? He hoped not. Big Ed dismissed this idea too. His son wasn't dead. Maybe he was just shacked up in a hotel room with some bimbo and was too wasted to realize where he left his car.

Hoping against hope, Big Ed turned from his view to answer a call that buzzed on his phone. It was the mayor. Maybe he had some news. Anxiously snatching up the receiver, Big Ed barked a hello.

"I just wanted to reassure you that everything is being done to find Carrington," Wallace told him without preamble.

"Does Warren have any leads?" Big Ed was anxious to hear anything the police may have found about his missing son. He had called police Chief Warren Allen earlier to learn he was out of the office; hopefully pursuing his son's disappearance.

"I'm sorry to say there doesn't seem to be a trace of him anywhere. It's as if he vanished into thin air. Are you sure he just didn't run off with some girl and doesn't want to be found?" Wallace believed Carrington would show up unharmed after recovering from one of his many drug induced escapades. He was known to the police department for his pain in the ass clashes with the law. If not for Big Ed, he would have been locked away years ago.

Big Ed shook his head as if Wallace could see the gesture. "I wouldn't be worried if his car hadn't been found abandoned. You know how he treasures that car."

Wallace had to agree. Carrington's sole purpose in life was to covet that car above anything else. It was as much a tool as it was a prized possession, by enabling him to draw the many women he was known to collect like trophies.

"Don't worry old friend. Warren has everything under control. But because of the elections, we can't conduct the usually head busting to get quick answers, so it will be a little slow going.

Big Ed nodded his head in agreement. He knew what was at stake. He loved his son, but he understood the risks. None of them needed any heat right now if they wanted to stay in power. And although his family wasn't in need of the money, the high he gained from their operations was by far unmatched. He craved the exhilaration of it all. He was addicted. Once they added the latest element to the list of their dirty deeds, it was like achieving a spiritual awakening. Who knew human trafficking could be so stimulating. Although he wasn't directly involved in this part of the business, it still had its perks; thanks to the generosity of their newest business partner. Big Ed's penis grew at the mere thought of those perks.

After assuring Wallace that he understood the circumstances, Big Ed ended the call. He just hoped they would find his son soon and alive. But in the meantime, he needed to relax. He was wound up way too tight to get anything done. Picking up the phone again, he dialed a private number. He needed a stress reliever for the evening.

Chapter 5

Mason Coburn inspected the girls Reese had led into the common room of the warehouse. There were twelve in all, just like the other shipments. Reese watched as he ran a finger down the side of one of the girl's cheeks. She wanted to hurry him along, but stopped herself from verbalizing this desire. Although she wasn't one of his girls, she wouldn't take the chance on being the object of his wrath. She'd witnessed what he was capable of when he was angry. One of the girls from a previous shipment had the misfortune to experience that anger first hand, after she spit in his face when he touched her. Reese had watched as Coburn calmly cleaned his face with his expensive handkerchief, before beating the girl senseless. After word spread about Coburn's temper, there wasn't another incident.

Mason Coburn was Mayor Wallace's good friend and newest business partner. Reese thought they were doing quite well without adding Coburn's sorted trade to their already profitable ventures. Dealing in prostitution made Reese uneasy, especially since these girls— barely out of their teens—were unwilling participants. But Riley said Coburn, along with his special enterprise, was there to stay. He said the bosses were thrilled by the added venture. Not only were they benefitting from the added revenue, they were using some of the girls for their own personal pleasures. When she asked how Wallace knew Coburn, Riley had laughed, stating they met in church. This made Reese shiver.

After inspecting the last girl, Coburn nodded. "These will do for now, but the next shipment will have to be better. I'll speak to my contact to make sure of it."

Reese released a breath she hadn't realized she was holding. She understood what that meant. The girls were pretty, but they weren't up to his usual standards. Coburn's girls were all high class; top of the line. He said street walkers were the ones who landed you in prison, because they were unpredictable and hard to handle. Because this shipment didn't quite fulfill his agenda for his high dollar clientele, they would be exchanging the girls sooner than usual.

They had a system. Each new shipment of girls was placed in-service for exactly one month, before they were exchanged for a new batch. They didn't need to keep them any longer than that. One of the reasons being, Coburn's clients became easily bored and demanded variety. But the main reason involved staying ahead of the authorities. Even though they had most of Metro City's police department in their pocket, it didn't do well to draw any unnecessary attention from other law enforcement agencies, not to mention the overzealous detectives who weren't involved in the mayor's backroom deals.

After watching the last of the girls loaded onto a van that would take them to their new home, Father Mason Coburn reattached his collar. It was time he headed back to the rectory to prepare for evening mass.

Chapter 6

Kobe casually tapped the table top as he considered his new partner. He was waiting for KT to return from the ladies room, in what had become his favorite restaurant. They had decided to meet for lunch to compare notes on the case. After their meeting the night before, he decided to read up on his new partner and what he found was extraordinary.

Although KT mentioned her work in Special Operations, she failed to mention the commendations she received for that work. She and Tor both were highly sought after leaving the army, and had received offers from various intelligence agencies around the world. The two, along with three others, worked classified assignments for military intelligence, with Tor heading the decorated team. Kobe discovered, upon leaving his post with the army, Tor worked a brief stint for Anderson Stone, his boss' brother in law, before choosing to go it alone; making KT one of his first hires, the moment he opened his investigative firm. And from there, Tor continued cultivating his organization into one of the top investigative agencies in the country.

Kobe met Tor briefly when returning from leave after Bria's death. After Bria was killed, he left Jamaica without so much as a backward glance; wanting nothing more to do with the case against Romaro Grey or his crew. After meeting Tor, he discovered he was instrumental in learning Grey's responsibility for Pilar Mendez's fate. Pilar was Matthias' wife Sienna's mother. He and Bria, along with Matthias, were working on Sienna's case in Jamaica when Bria was gunned down. After Matthias' and Sienna's wedding, Matthias moved his headquarters to Metro City, giving his employees the option to come with him. Since Kobe had no family to speak of, he jumped at the chance to make a fresh start.

After learning of Tor and KT's accomplishments, he read up on the other key members of Tor's operation. Maalik Wyatt, although not military, was on top of his game as well. Maalik was instrumental in breaking the case on who was trying to kill Justin Graham, head of Graham Inc.; another former client of Tor's. Maalik did a brief stint with the local police department, before deciding he wasn't cut out for such a structured organization. Metro PD's loss was Tor Hudson's gain. And the last hired was a man by the name of Brody Grimes. Although military, Brody was an ex-marine who Tor met after leaving the armed forces.

Brody was considered the most conservative of the group. Whereas the others were quicker to act, Brody took the time to evaluate ever angle before proceeding. He was known best for his communicative tactics to bring about peaceful solutions to difficult situations.

The more he read about Tor's operation and abilities, and that of his team, the more he began to relax. He was equally impressed with how KT handled herself, especially during the Graham case. He found she was more than capable to get the job done. Kobe breathed a sigh of relief. He didn't have to worry about KT falling down on her duties.

Kobe frowned. This last thought disturbed him. It implied that Bria had neglected her duties and had gotten herself killed. This was far from the truth and he knew. But why had he viewed it that way? He concluded it was just a slip of the mind. He was tired is all. He had yet to get a decent night's sleep. He sighed again. He may have to look into other methods of relaxation in order to get some rest. Matthias had been pushing him to see someone to help handle his still lingering grief. If he didn't sleep soon he was afraid he would have to.

"So what's good to eat here?" KT had returned to their table.

"Everything here at Mama Anna's is good; that's if you like down home Louisiana cooking. I guess I should have asked before I suggested this place." He hadn't thought she may not like Cajun and Creole food.

Perusing the menu, KT answered him. "One thing about me Kobe, I love food, any food. So yes, Louisiana food is fine. How about the seafood gumbo?"

Kobe smiled. "Excellent choice and one of my favorites. You won't be disappointed." He handed the server his menu after placing his order. After the server left, he felt the need to make small talk. He knew all about KT's professional life; he wanted to know more about the woman.

"Why does everyone call you KT instead of Kaitlin?" He thought Kaitlin suited her much better.

"I learned early on in life that females were looked upon in a certain way and if I wanted to be taken seriously I had to make some changes. I became KT after joining the army. I wanted to literally be all I could be and not be just another female in the military. So to rise in the ranks and in the minds of my peers, I became KT. And just like you, most men automatically assume I'm a man. Then that brings a whole new set of issues when they find out I'm not…that is until they hear my resume, then the respect comes." KT watched Kobe's demeanor. She hit the nail on the head. "So, I guess you had me checked out." She smiled at his discomfort.

"Ok I must admit, I had some reservations but yes I checked you out."

"I take it you don't know Tor personally because if you did, you would know he only hires the best."

Kobe shook his head. "No I don't know him that well. I've only met your boss once. It was after Jamaica." Kobe was quiet. For a moment he had forgotten about Bria and that hadn't settled right with him. He felt he needed to keep her in the fore front of his mind. He owed her that much.

As if reading his mind, KT responded. "You can let go of your grief without forgetting her you know. Kobe I've done some reading on you too. It wasn't your fault Bria died. You weren't the one who shot her. How were you to know that fool would open fire without warning?

From what I understand, she wasn't the only one hit that day." Two of the islands police officers sustained wounds from Romero Grey's rampage. Bria was the only one to die.

"I just feel as if there had to be something I could have done. Something…" Kobe didn't need a shrink to tell him he was being irrational. How could he have foreseen this? None of the rescue party saw it coming. He was just as surprised as everyone else when those shots rang out.

Kobe swiped a hand down his face. He believed if he let go of what happened, he would be letting go of Bria. But he realized KT was right. He could never forget her, never.

They tabled the discussion while they ate their meal, only making small talk and filling in the blanks on the investigation. They were just about to map a game plan for surveillance when KT's phone rang.

Chapter 7

Brody Grimes rubbed his palm over his closely cropped hair. He had been trying to reach his brother all afternoon to no avail. When he called his home, the phone just continued to ring, so he decided to drop by. He rang the doorbell but no one answered. The garage door was up and both his brother's and sister in-law's cars were parked there. He glanced along the quiet street where a car, he didn't recognize, was parked at the curb in front of the house.

Brody peered through the front windows into the living room and dining room. There was no sign of the couple. Deciding something could be wrong, he walked around to the back of the house to peer through the windows there. He just hoped he wouldn't stumble upon an eye full of his brother and his wife doing the do.

He dismissed this idea with a shake of his head. Tony was supposed to meet him for a late lunch and it was unlike him to blow him off without a phone call. When he made his way around to the master suite, he couldn't believe what he was seeing. Lynette was sitting in a chair holding a gun on his brother and some woman. Both Tony and the woman were naked and cowering on the bed. Brody groaned. Lynette had finally caught Tony cheating.

Taking his phone from his pocket, Brody punched in a number before making his way back to the front of the house. He was going to need some help.

***

KT's eyes widened as she listened to her colleague's predicament. He didn't go into much detail, but what he did tell her, had her alarmed. Brody's brother was being held at gun point by his wife.

Grabbing up her notes, KT shoved them into her carrier bag. "I hate to cut this short but I need to make a run…you know what, scratch that. *We* need to make a run," she reconsidered. If Kobe was going to be her partner, there was no better time than to start now. "Come on, we might need your help." KT directed this to a curious Kobe. They had just finished lunch and were laying out a plan for their assignment.

"What's wrong?" he asked; shoving his notepad and phone into his back pocket.

"I'll fill you in on the way." KT was concerned. For Brody to call her for help and not the police, meant he wanted to keep this as an in-house issue. She just hoped they wouldn't need any more help. Tor was working another case across town and Maalik was out of the country on vacation with his girlfriend Dani Sinclair.

Chapter 8

Lynette Grimes sat backwards in one of her dining room chairs, as she watched her husband and his mistress cower on her king sized bed. Actually the mistress was doing more of the cowering. Her husband, on the other hand, may have been surprised, but he wasn't huddled in fear, like his bed partner. After the initial shock of being caught, he was just as cool as ever.

Dismissing her husband for the moment, she focused her gaze on the woman. Lynette pursed her lips with distain. The bitch had the nerve to act modest, with *her* favorite sheets pulled up to her chin; trying desperately to cover her double D breasts. So is that it? The huge knockers? Is that what turns Tony on?

Lynette had dragged the ornate chair into the bedroom from the eloquently decorated dining room. It had taken her months to choose the perfect colors and cushion pattern for the set. All of that was forgotten as she took her time leaving drag marks on the pristine flooring leading to the master suite. It didn't matter if she mangled the chair's legs; she was on a mission. She wasn't in any hurry to make her destination. Why should she be? It took time to remain calm and controlled while she chewed over what to do about the pair holed up in her equally eloquent bedroom.

When she finally reached the master suite, she stopped and stood just inside the doorway to take in the revolting sight. They were grunting and carrying on so, they hadn't heard her enter the house let alone the bedroom. That was until she closed the door with a resounding bang, grabbing both of their attentions.

Lynette watched Tony pull out of the bimbo so fast he nearly fell from the bed. She also noticed, when he whipped around, he didn't even have the sense to wear a condom. He was riding this bitch raw. Lynette's eyes narrowed with contempt, as she sat down on the chair watching them. She made a mental note to make an appointment with her doctor.

"Lynette… what…?" Tony hesitated, not knowing how to proceed.

Lynette's eyebrows rose. "What am I doing here?" She asked; finishing the sentence for him. Lynette tilted her head with wonder at this foolishness. "I live here or did you forget once you started banging this brainless bimbo?" Lynette spoke with a deadly calm. So deadly and so calm, she would have thought the woman in her bed would've had the good sense to keep her mouth shut.

"Now wait a minute bitch, who you calling a brainless bimbo? I have you to know I have a Doctorate in Science," the woman snidely informed Lynette. She was so angry that she'd forgotten she was trying to hide those double damned implants and had let the sheets fall to her waist. She even had the nerve to give Lynette a sista-girl neck roll in defiance.

Without saying another word, Lynette reached around to the small of her back; wasting no time in producing a hand gun, she had tucked in her waistband, to level at the irate woman. Closing her mouth with an audible snap, Dr. Science started back peddling towards the headboard.

"That's more like it. The less said by *you* the better," Lynette told the wide eyed woman, in her still calm and easy voice.

"Lynette!" Tony's eyes grew with the sight of the gun. "What are you doing?" Even he started pushing back; trying to place as much distance between himself and her now visible hand gun.

"I'm leveling the playing field Tony…don't you think it's about time? Lynette gave him all the attitude she felt in a satisfied smirk.

Lynette's smug satisfaction irritated Tony. He had had just about enough of this scene. He understood she was angry, but she had made her point. Now it was time for her to get over it and move on.

"Level the…listen, I can explain!" Tony readjusted his line of approach and decided to try to explain himself, instead of verbally attacking her. He was aggravated, but not heated enough to rile Lynette; not in this current situation. He knew his wife. Whenever problems came up, she just needed a little reassurance and he was always handy to give it to her. He thought if he could try to explain things, she would calm down. His mind skidded to a stop on this thought. Calm down? He had to rethink this. The woman was already beyond calm and that concerned him. He had never experienced this Lynette before.

Lynette lifted a corner of her painted mouth into a half smile. *Isn't that what they all said? I can explain? As far as I'm concerned, there is nothing to explain. I came home to find my loving husband banging this double D bitch—end of story. What more could he possibly add to this scenario? Maybe he wanted to explain the many positions he had this trick in my bed! Oh wait! Maybe he wanted to explain how he bounced those fake titties around, while he was hitting it doggy style. Hum, this should be interesting*, Lynette thought with an even bigger grin.

Slowly Tony inched forward to sit back on his hunches. Lynette hadn't shot him yet, so he thought he would try talking to her. As he drew in a deep calculating breath, he could feel the bed vibrating from Cassie's fear. He wouldn't dare turn to look at her. He tried not to think about her at that moment. He didn't want to give his wife a reason—as if she didn't already have one—to shoot him. His focus needed to be on Lynette and Lynette only—and her gun.

"Listen Lynette…"

Chapter 9

Tony couldn't believe he was in this predicament. Here he was in their bed with his mistress, all while his wife pointed a very big and very capable gun at them. He was trying to wrap his mind around how this happened. He thought he had been so careful. He had been banging Cassie for nearly a year without any suspicion or breach of marital protocol. He was always home on time for dinner—whenever Lynette decided to cook—or any other planned event that if ignored, may have roused attention. Well at least up until lately. But his absence was easily explained away by his campaign in gaining a seat in the state house.

As he gathered his thoughts, he ran over the remainder of his checklist. Everything was in order except for today. Lynette never came home in the middle of the day, never. This is why he was so comfortable in inviting Cassie to their home. In the early years of their marriage, he tried many times to get her to meet him for a noon day romp in the sack, but she always declined. She always claimed that she loved him too much to settle for a quickie. He concluded that she was more dedicated to her duties as an elementary school teacher than she was to his needs. So what brought her home today? Did she forget something this morning or did she suspect? Considering she brought a gun, Tony chose the latter. But if she suspected, how? What gave him away?

Tony racked his mind to answer the annoying question. There wasn't a time when Lynette couldn't reach him. He always took her calls, whether at the office or not. Hell, there was a time when he answered the phone with his hand covering Cassie's mouth, even as he pounded away inside her. He never missed a stroke. He always showered before he came home; never leaving a trace of anything incriminating. Until recently, he played the part of the dutiful husband by sending her flowers and gifts to appease her. Was that it? Because he stopped sending her flowers? Tony mental pounded his head. He stared back at his wife. He knew he had to come up with something soon, because he could tell she was becoming impatient.

Here goes nothing. Drawing in a ragged breath, Tony spoke. "Lynette, first of all I'm sorry. I know it's nowhere close to enough to say that, but I truly am sorry. You're my wife and I had no right to defile our marriage like this. I don't know what made me take this route. I can't blame middle age crisis or any shit like that. Hell, I am only thirty seven years old." Tony chuckled at this; trying to lighten the mood in the room. But he took one look at Lynette's face and the laughter died in his throat. She was not amused. And from the quickening vibration of the bed, neither was Cassie.

Clearing his throat he pressed on. "Anyway, I guess I don't have a real excuse, but I can tell you, Cassie here means nothing to me. She was a bad mistake that I will be spending the rest of my life making up to you. I love you...I never stopped loving you. Baby, this," he boldly gestured toward the bed and a surprised Cassie, "is all a mistake and you have my word it will never happen again."

Tony stared at his wife. He hoped it was enough. He knew it all sounded cliché, but he couldn't clear his mind enough to come up with anything better. Usually, when it came to explanations and smoothing things over, whether in the courtroom or with his wife, he was running at one hundred percent. But Lynette was right. That gun was an equalizer. It prevented him from being his usual condescending self.

"YOU SON OF A BITCH!" This was from Cassie; shattering all the calm in the room. With Lynette and her gun forgotten, she let the sheets go altogether. She was furious. She sat there seething as she listened to Tony throw her under the bus; distancing himself from his culpability in this mess. He spoke of her as if she were some cheap tramp he picked up and had a one-time fling with.

Struggling within the tangled bedding to get to her knees, she hauled off and slapped him. "What the hell do you mean, I mean nothing to you?! That's not what you've been telling me for the past year. You fucking bastard!" Cassie continued to pummel a now cowering Tony, until Lynette interceded.

"ENOUGH!" At her booming voice, Tony and Cassie's heads whipped around, both fully expecting to hear gunshots ring out next. This was the most emotion Lynette had displayed since entering the bedroom.

"So this little dance has been going on for a year." This was a statement. Lynette had suspected it had been going on for awhile, but had no idea it had been that long. This was truly an eye opener for her. She would have to rethink some things.

Tony closed his eyes and inwardly groaned. Placing his hands in a praying stance against his face, he had to think. If only Cassie had kept her mouth shut, he could have possibly led them out of this mess.

Taking a chance, he cut his eyes at Cassie. Tony wanted to strangle her. Sure he said he loved her and wanted to be with her, but that was the party line. It's not his fault the silly bitch believed him. He loved his wife as much as any man loved his wife. There is no way he was leaving Lynette, at least not for Cassie. She was just a distraction until he reached his true goal. Cassie was fun and thrills in bed, but Lynette was his stepping stone; his ticket. He had purposely and meticulously married and built a life with her; a life he had no intentions of giving up until he was ready. His gaze swung back to Lynette. Well, he hadn't any intentions of leaving her *yet*, but with this little situation, staying may not be a possibility. He needed to fix this and fast.

Chapter 10

Lynette's heart rate increased. She was furious. She'd only become suspicious of an affair a couple of months ago. She just assumed she was only a month behind this, not an entire year. She narrowed her eyes at this revelation. Could she be that stupid to not know Tony was screwing around for a year and not catch on?

Her first hint that something was wrong was when his assistant asked if she liked the gift Tony sent her. She had come to take him to lunch and was engaging in small talk with Brenda while she waited for him to return from court. She didn't want to appear dense, so she played along and told the woman she loved it. She had never received any damn gift! In fact, she hadn't received anything from Tony in quite some time.

Now, looking back on the exchange, Lynette wondered if the woman was trying to tell her all along. There was no way she could have made that mistake, seeing as she would have been the one to place the order. Brenda, Tony's assistant had only been working with him for a few months and she and Lynette were just getting to know each other. Lynette made a mental note to buy the woman anything she wanted. It wasn't her fault she missed her obvious hint.

The real clue came when she found a bank receipt on the bathroom floor, after Tony had left for work one morning. Because she and Tony managed two joint accounts together, she never had a reason to look into his personal account. But when she started investigating, she found, a part from their joint accounts and there agreed upon individual personal accounts, he had several other accounts; three to be exact.

When they were first married, they each agreed that a part from the mutual household accounts, they would maintain a separate account for their personal use. They each had their own little vices. She liked to shop for shoes and clothes, and he liked his video games and golf. Tony was a video game fanatic and bought all the sports and other popular games that were available. Lynette never thought he would use the account for anything other than that. But after discovering his other accounts, she wondered about other vices; the ones she knew nothing about. She kept digging until she came across hotel and restaurant receipts, along with receipts for various cash deposits and withdrawals. Tony was spending thousands of dollars;

some of which was spent on jewelry, a mustang convertible and a mortgage for a condo they didn't own. Although the discovery of the affair was enough, she was curious to know where all the extra money was coming from. Where two of the accounts only held a few hundred, one off shore account, held close to two million dollars.

She promised herself she would keep digging until she found the source, but at the time, she was more concerned about the affair. She had agonized over her discovery for weeks, but kept her composure just the same. Who was this woman he was sneaking around with and how was she going to find out? She got her chance when she overheard Tony's phone conversation, asking the woman to meet him at the house for an early lunch. She could tell it wasn't business by the way he spoke to her. It was the same voice he used when he was in the mood and wanted to get busy. She wondered how many 'lunches' had they had in their home.

Lynette knew it had come time for her to confront her husband on his duplicity. Never once letting on that she knew, she got up that morning as usual. She cooked breakfast and kissed him goodbye as they both headed off to work. But Lynette didn't go to work. She detoured to visit a friend to get her head together, in order to ready herself for this confrontation. With the help of her friend, Lynette had calmed herself to the point of acceptance. She had never been one of those females who stuck her head in the sand; pretending nothing was happening. She was the meet it head-on type and meet it head-on was what she did.

She retrieved her gun from its hidden spot in her closet and placed it in her purse after breakfast. She never intended to use it, just scare the hell out of her cheating husband. He had to learn that he couldn't cross her and get away with it. But that was before she learned how long the affair had been going on.

Contrary to what Tony tried to lead her to believe, he had been with this woman for a year. In Lynette's mind, meeting a couple of times a month was a fling, but seeing this woman on a regular basis for a year was a relationship, whether he wanted to admit it or not. Before this revelation, she thought she had this thing figured out. She would scream and curse, he would say he was sorry and promise to never do it again and they would move on. But this was a game changer. She had to rethink some things. She had to.

Chapter 11

"So what's the situation?" KT asked Brody the moment he met them at the end of the driveway. "Oh, by the way this is Kobe West from Matthias Bennett's firm. Kobe…Brody." The two men nodded at each other. Kobe recognized Brody from his dossier.

"Lynette is holding a gun on Tony and some woman. It looks like she came home to find them in the act."

"This can't be good," Kobe commented. "What do want to do?" he asked Brody.

"Luckily I have a key to the house. I'm going to go inside and see if I can talk her down. I won't be able to enter the room because she's posted herself in a chair against the door. I want you two to go around back and be my eyes." KT and Kobe nodded and left to head around back.

Brody shook his head at this turn of events. Tony had always been an ass. He had been cheating on Lynette for years and he found it amazing that she hadn't found out before now. He often felt sorry for his sister in-law; she deserved better. But because Tony was his brother, Brody vowed to stay out of his marriage. He told himself it wasn't any of his business. But after what he witnessed today, he wondered if he made the right call. If Lynette killed Tony it would be his fault.

Making his way back into the house again, Brody went over what he should say to Lynette. He hated Tony for putting her in this position. He'd always like Lynette and knew she could've done better than Tony. His brother was selfish, bordering on narcissism; always implying that whatever he desired was his for the taking. Brody knew Tony never loved Lynette. She just looked good on paper while he built his political career. Lynette was smart, attractive and savvy, everything Tony needed to catapult him to his goal—state governor.

Reaching the bedroom door, Brody knocked. "Lynette?"

Tony nearly passed out from relief at hearing his brother's voice. He had come to save him. He knew once he didn't show up at the restaurant and didn't call, Brody would come to the house. He just hoped he could talk Lynette into putting that gun down so he could gain control; something that, up until now, had always been his territory, not Lynette's. After learning of the length of his affair, he saw a visual change in her and it wasn't for the better. Until this point, Lynette had been calm, but that was about to go to hell from the way she gripped the handle of the Beretta.

"Not now Brody. Your brother and I have some things to work out, so I would appreciate it if you just left us alone." Lynette was not happy to hear her brother in-law's voice on the other side of the door. She didn't need him interfering. She realized now that she wanted satisfaction, and satisfaction for her was to put a bullet in her lying cheating husband.

"Lynette, you know I can't do that. If fact, I would feel better if you would put the gun down so you and I could talk. I don't want you to accidently hurt someone." Brody hoped she would lay the gun aside and just focus on him, and not the occupants in the room. Usually he was in his element. Getting people to talk and persuading them to listen to his solutions was his thing. But this was family and he didn't know how effective he could be under the circumstances.

"Oh believe me Brody, it won't be by accident." Lynette stared hard at Tony. She wondered what else he'd been up to. And where did all that money come from? Her focus shifted when she saw movement at the French doors that lead to the patio. "Brody, did you bring company?" she should have known he wouldn't have come alone. She thought she saw a shadow of someone earlier but dismissed it. Now she knew it had to be Brody.

"Yes I did. We all want this to end peacefully. I know Tony has been a tool, but you must understand, if you kill him, he wins by completely ruining your life. I know you love him and you didn't deserve this, but why destroy yourself by hurting him? You know I love you both and I don't want to see this end badly. So come on and open the door and let me in. I will help you sort everything out."

While he waited for an answer, Brody tried the door handle. It was locked. He pulled his knife from its sheath attached to his belt, hoping to pry the lock free. He thought if he could just ease the door open a little, he could persuade her to let him come inside.

Lynette shifted her gaze from Tony to Cassie. She was shaking like a leaf. She wanted to laugh at her fear, but stopped herself. She wanted to know if she knew Tony was married when all of this began. She quickly dismissed this.

Even if she did know, she wasn't the problem. Tony knew he was married and chose to cheat anyway.

Lynette gestured with the Beretta. "Put your clothes on." Tony made a move to reach for his pants. Lynette refocused her gaze and her gun on him. "Not you, Cassie." She decided to let her off the hook.

Listening to the exchange, Brody held his position in the hallway, as did KT and Kobe outside.

Cassie only hesitated a second before scrambling from the bed to grab her clothes. She refused to take the time to think about what this could mean. She figured if Lynette was going to kill her, she would have done so already. Finished with pulling on her clothes, she waited for Lynette's next instructions; instructions she hoped would involve her leaving from that room alive.

"Hey! You people out there...my husband's skank is coming out!" Lynette smirked at Cassie's sullen reaction. She couldn't resist taking one last jab at the woman; she was sleeping with her husband.

Lynette motioned for Cassie to leave through the French doors that led out onto the patio; the patio that held the beautiful outdoor furniture she had imported just for that spot; the patio where she and Tony used to have leisurely Sunday brunches together. Now that was all over; Tony made sure of that.

Cassie, fully dressed, except for one shoe she couldn't find, snatched up her purse and keys from the floor and almost ran for the ornate doors. As soon as she released the lock, the door flew open and she was pulled through by KT. After she was taken to safety, she fell to her knees in hysterics. She didn't think she would make it out with her life.

When Cassie cleared the door, Lynette turned her attention back to her husband who was staring at her anxiously. She smiled. She knew he was wondering if he would be so lucky to walk out without harm.

"Lynette? Have you put the gun down?" Brody asked. KT informed him that Cassie was safe. He gave small thanks that she let the woman go. He now needed to talk her into letting his brother do the same. Placing the knife back into its sheath, he decided not to force his way in. He had faith Lynette would do the right thing. Brody believed she was hurt by his brother's betrayal, but not homicidal.

Tears streamed down Lynette's face. Her emotions had finally gotten the best of her. "Give me a reason why I shouldn't just put him down like a rabid dog. I loved him. I thought we were happy together. Did you know he's been cheating on me with that…that…for a year? Did you know that?" Lynette's calm was coming unraveled. Her hope for reconciliation was not an option now. Tony had a relationship not a fling. For her, it meant Tony cared about this woman; he had an emotional relationship with her. And as far as she was concerned, the marriage was over. So why should he come away unscathed? She hadn't.

"Listen Lynette. My brother is a bastard I know, but you are better than this; you deserve better than this. But if you don't put the gun down and walk away, you won't have a chance to find better. Do you hear me? There is someone out there who will treat you better; I promise." *Like you perhaps?*

Brody's conscience spoke up then. Deep down he loved Lynette and not as a sister, but as a woman. When he first met her, he knew she deserved more than Tony's casual feelings. She was too good for him. As the years progressed, and the more time he spent around her, he wanted her. He had been suppressing his feelings for her for years. He hoped now that she knew what type of man her husband was, maybe Lynette would look at him; really see him as the man she deserved. The man who would love her to no end.

Brody shook the wayward thought away. He shouldn't think like that. He couldn't go after his brother's wife. Could he? The click of the lock brought him back to his senses. She was coming out. Brody stepped back to let her pass. But to his surprise, she didn't walk passed him, she fell into his arms sobbing. Brody held her close as she let go of her pain. Closing his eyes, he struggled to resist the urge to kiss away her tears.

Once Lynette lowered the gun and stepped out into the hallway, Tony allowed himself to fall back onto the pillows with relief. His crazy bitch of a wife had finally given up. Maybe it was better that she knew, he thought. Besides, she had served her purpose. He was about to become a newly elected state representative, thanks to his friends in low places.

This first stepping stone into politics was just the start of something bigger for him. His greater ambition was to become governor; then who knows, maybe even president. But the key was always with Lynette. She possessed a character and class that he needed. And it didn't hurt that both of her parents were retired military. All which he used to build his platform in his run for state representative. Even though she was upset now, he knew she still loved him and would get past this little bump in the road.

Tony grinned. One way or the other, he would talk Lynette into keeping her mouth shut about the affair. And as for keeping the police out of what had taken place today, that was a non-issue thanks to his brother. Brody may not like him at the moment, but he wouldn't do anything to get his beloved Lynette in trouble. He almost laughed out loud. His brother was a fool. He knew Brody had the hots for his wife, no matter how hard he tried to hide it. And without the collaboration from him and Lynette, no one would believe Cassie, even if she ever decided to talk.

Now, he just had to get through the next few days without scandal, and he would be well on his way to his goal; today state representative, tomorrow the White House. Smugly, he rested his hands behind his head. Nothing could stop him now, nothing.

"Are you ok?" KT asked Tony. He hadn't heard her enter the room. He had gotten so comfortable in his fantasy of becoming president he'd forgotten the very recent life and death situation he narrowly escaped.

"I'm fine. Could you hand me my pants?" Sitting up, he grinned up at KT, while he casually stroked himself. Just thinking about his destiny had given him a hard on.

KT frowned. She couldn't believe the man. His wife could have killed him and he was sitting there playing with himself and grinning like an idiot. She wondered just who was Tony Grimes. He was nothing like his brother. Although relieved that all turned out well for all involved, she shook her head at him. It really wouldn't have served any purpose if Lynette had killed them. KT knew she was hurting, but it was time to make him hurt by taking everything from him; starting with the coveted seat for the state house. If it were her, she would be telling the world what a lying piece of crap he was. Shaking her head again, she left to join the others outside.

Chapter 12

Police Chief Warren Allen narrowed his eyes at what his sergeant was telling him. One of his neighborhood 'employees' had come up short with the week's take. This was the second time—in as many months—the man hadn't produced what he owed. This was a habit he would have to put a stop to and soon. But if he addressed the problem now, there might be trouble and the mayor didn't want any type of trouble just before the elections.

Riley Phillips watched a vein pulsate in his boss's forehead. He felt his frustration. Terrance "Ice" James was playing them and everyone knew. He saw the opportunity and he took full advantage of it. Ice waited with precision timing to run his nobody is buying game.

His claim that the local ministers were rounding up the usual buyers, convincing them to enter their rehab programs instead of getting high, was a straight up lie. Everyone knew it was a lie before he could get it out of his mouth good. The preachers may have talked a good game about removing blight and corruption from the streets, but their main game was stuffing more loot into their pockets via government subsidies. They placed just enough bodies in those facilities to keep the checks rolling in without doling out a cent from their own coffers. And what they called rehab facilities were little more than a few rundown houses managed by retired nurses. Often leading to their clientele returning to the streets and their habits with a vengeance.

Ice was a problem Riley wanted free reign to put a stop to. He was just waiting for the Chief to give him the ok, so he and his boys could put an end to him once and for all.

"Shit!" Allen slammed his fist down on his desk. "That little bastard thinks he has things all figured out. He's banking on me not touching his ass before the mayor is re-elected." Allen swiped a palm across his face. If it wasn't for the mayor, he would handle it today. He didn't give a shit if Terrance was his wife's nephew. Business was business no matter whose blood ran through his veins. He would take out his own mama if she got in the way of his earnings.

"What do you want me to do about him?" Phillips was anxious. He hoped the Chief would give him the green light to put him down. Nothing would give him more pleasure. He hated Terrance James; hated him, because he was responsible for the death of the only woman who ever loved him.

"How much was he short this time?" Allen asked.

"Twenty grand."

"Son of a…" The vein in Allen's head pulsed more. "That bastard has been stealing from us all along…I just know it!" Allen rested his head on his joined hands. He had to think. If they didn't deal with this fool now, they would have a mutiny on their hands. All the other dealers would think they could get away with stiffing them too.

Abruptly sitting up in his chair, Allen rubbed his chin. "Let me make a phone call and I'll get back to you." Allen picked up the phone once Phillips left his office.

***

Riley Phillips' jaw clenched as he left the Chief's office. He was rearing to get his hands on Ice. If it hadn't been for the Chief, he would have killed him years ago. That bastard had a lot to answer for.

"So what did he say?" This was from Teddy Reid, one of Phillips' men. Three of his subordinates were crowded around the assignment board, anticipating their next move. Things had been quiet and they were more than ready to bust some heads.

"He'll get back to me." This was all Riley said before entering his office to calm himself. Closing the door behind him, he sat at his desk and pulled Nadia's photo from a drawer. Placing a fingertip to the photo, he traced her smiling face. He missed her deeply. She was the love of his life. She was the one woman who looked beyond his plain, drab exterior to touch his soul. He had never met a woman who came close to his beautiful Nadia.

Nadia Perez died two years prior; just days before they were to be married. She was downtown picking up her wedding dress when Ice and one of his fellow gangbangers decided to rob one of the merchants near the shop. After taking all the money the shop owner had, they sprinted from the store, joyful over their take and how easy it was to take it. But it wasn't as easy as they thought, because the store owner followed them outside with a shotgun. But instead of hitting one of the men who robbed him, the man pulled the trigger the moment Nadia walked into his line of fire. The blast took half her face off, killing her instantly.

Riley blamed Ice for her death. If he had been following the Chief's rule of no outside activities, Nadia would still be alive. And because the shop owner was the only witness to the robbery and the goods weren't ever found, Ice walked without spending a day in jail. Some said he got off because he was the Chief's nephew. But Ice's activities that day hadn't sat well with the Chief either. Had it been up to him, and not the prosecutor he would have thrown Ice up under the jail, wife's wishes or not.

Placing the photo back into the drawer, Riley ground his teeth some more. Now that money was in play, he wondered if the Chief regretted his decision in not taking care of Ice after Nadia's death. It seemed to him, money was always more important to the bosses than an innocent life. Never the less, he hoped this would be the motivator to get the job done.

Riley vacated his chair to pace his office. He had waited two long years for that fool to screw up and he didn't want to wait a moment longer. Riley Phillips wanted Ice to die a slow and painful death as soon as possible.

Chapter 13

Mayor Craven Wallace leaned back in his expensive handcrafted leather chair; a chair he had grown very fond of. He was about to embark on his third term as mayor of his fine city, and he was thrilled. He thought of it as his city, because he considered himself as king; able to do whatever, whenever he wanted. And what he wanted was more time and opportunity to fatten his offshore bank account.

Since becoming mayor, he had made more money in a few short years than he would have been able to make his entire lifetime in the streets. Craven was able to make his dreams come true due to his handpicked right hand man, police Chief Warren Allen. He'd know Allen since their days of running the neighborhood crack houses and corners. He and Allen ruled the 87th Dog Street Mob. He shook his head at the memory. Those were the days; days he was happy to put behind him, thanks to his favorite priest.

Craven Wallace had been legit on paper for fifteen years with the help of Father Coburn, his old neighborhood's parish priest. Father Coburn had taken

Craven under his wing, seeing a potential in him that the good Father claimed only God could command. Craven was amused at how naïve Father Coburn had been back then; thinking he could save the world. He thanked the Father just the same, because if it hadn't been for him, he probably would be spending his days in prison, if not the grave. And it would have been a shame to have missed out on all of the great opportunities that his new life now afforded him.

Not only had Craven made good by becoming Metro City's mayor, but he had managed to parlay his criminal earnings into legitimate business ventures that netted him millions. Since becoming a part of the city's elite, he has lived the life he could only dream of when he was running street level with DSM. Never one to forget where he came from, Craven didn't overlook his fellow gangbangers. Once he took his first oath of office, he continued to manage them, by expanding on his illegal ventures in the old hood; netting him even more power and money. And with his very own tax payer funded muscle, handpicked from Metro City's finest, he was indeed king.

Swerving his chair around to look out on his fair city, from his seventh floor suite of offices, Craven's smile grew wide. In just over a couple of weeks he would win his third term in office. He was confident this would happen, because his plans were developing without a flaw. Thinking on his first term, it didn't bother him that he didn't have the backing he had in the first election. The way things were set up now, he didn't need them. He needed the people's backing in the first election just to get his foot in the door. After that, it was all window dressing.

The first election was a breeze. He ran on the platform of a reformed street thug, who, 'through much prayer and hard work', made great personal sacrifices to turn his life around. This well played deception was enforced due to Father Coburn standing by his side every step of the campaign. Everyone trusted a priest. With Coburn's credibility backing him, he fed the public his dreams of a better city for the less fortunate; the underdog; and the public ate it up. Everyone loved a feel good story of how a bad boy turned good.

The down trodden public fully embraced the new mayor, who came with brazen ideas that the people were eager to see to fruition. Although he implemented some of those ideas, some of his constituents felt he hadn't done enough and wanted him out. So to ensure he would rule a second term, he gave the process some under the table financial boosts. But in doing so, his efforts triggered suspicions that things may not have been on the up-in-up in the last election. To remedy this, he wouldn't be using the same tactics as before. While the AG would be looking for voter fraud amongst the masses of voters, this time he would be rigging the voting machines themselves. And to accomplish this, he hired just the man to do it—Tony Grimes; one of the brilliant minds in the district attorney's office, in exchange for sending him to the state house. Craven was impressed by Grimes' plan. In fact, he liked the idea so much he cut him in on some of his other ventures.

Craven turned from his musings when his private line buzzed. Reluctantly turning from his view, he answered the call. Before he could say hello, Chief Allen launched into his tirade.

"We have to do something about that scum Ice today!" Allen had had enough. They had to do something and do something now.

Craven sighed and pinched the bridge of his nose as he listened to his friend. Warren's nephew was out of control and he was right, something had to be done. Weighing out his options, Craven reluctantly gave him the green light to handle the matter. He agreed. If they didn't stop it now, they would have a bigger problem down the road.

"Just make sure it's done without any kind of blowback on us, you hear me!" Craven slammed down the phone. It was the wrong time for this foolishness. He just hoped his right hand could handle it quietly and without fail.

Chapter 14

Twenty-two year old Terrance "Ice" James threw his head back in ecstasy. Not only was he receiving the best head of his life, he had managed to squirrel away another twenty grand of his uncle's money. His joy widened when he envisioned the great Chief in a rage over the loss. He knew he probably wanted his head on a platter, but he didn't care. It was his time and there wasn't anything anyone could do about it. Besides, his Aunt Sadie wouldn't let anything happen to him. She loved him. She promised his dying mother that she would take care of him no matter what.

Ice released in the eighteen year old girl's mouth and pushed her away. He zipped up as the girl ran to the bathroom to spit out his load. Ice laughed. It was all good. He was breaking in a new one. He knew he should have taken the time to force her to swallow it, but he had more important things to attend to. He and his boys were going out to see what they could get into. Since he stopped pushing his uncle's drugs, he had a lot more free time on his hands. Instead of selling his goods to the junkies on the corners, he unloaded all of his supply to another dealer he knew at a hefty profit. Why work if you didn't have to?

Before he ventured out for the evening, Ice opened his safe to finger his insurance policy. This was his ritual each day to reassure himself that he still had the power. He had collected enough evidence against his uncle and that evil sidekick of his Craven Wallace, to put them away for a very long time. He knew eventually they would come after him, so he was prepared just in case Aunt Sadie couldn't stop them. And with all the money he'd taken, he knew the Chief wouldn't let his wife get in the way, not this time.

Ice laughed out loud when he thought about his uncle the Chief. That fool thought he had it all together; tied up in a neat little package. He stumbled upon the Chief's secret by accident. He had come to the warehouse, to pay his weekly homage, to discover his uncle and Wallace putting an end to someone. He was about to round the corner to the office, when he heard the mayor directing the poor soul to his knees just before ol' Uncle Warren put a bullet in the man's head. He grabbed his cell just in time to capture the moment on video. Getting what he needed, he quietly left the warehouse without being seen by either of them. He didn't know what it was all about then, but he was anxious to find out.

After a couple of days of quietly picking the brains of street creepers, he found out the man who was killed, was skimming guns from their shipments in order to sell on the side to the local bad-asses. And instead of having their favorite goon, Riley Phillips, take care of the problem, the Chief and Wallace decided to execute the problem themselves; sending a message to the other employees, that the bosses weren't to be trifled with.

After learning of this, Ice's wheels started turning and his plan began to form. Even though the hit was rumored to be carried out personally by the bosses, it could never be proven—or so everyone thought. With what he held, he could finally make some real money. And when his uncle finally did catch on and come for him, he held the keys to get out of jail, so to speak.

Assured that his insurance was safe, Ice placed his favorite ball cap on his head. He knocked on the bathroom door to hurry the girl along. It was time to pick up his crew.

Chapter 15

Riley stood behind Ice as he took a piss in one of the restroom's urinals. He had been waiting all night to get him alone. Teddy and the boys were waiting outside in the alley.

Ice had taken a break from the close crowd and pounding music of his favorite club. He and his crew had been holed up in the VIP section guzzling drinks and snorting cocaine for the better part of the night. Stumbling into the private restroom, Ice did another line of coke before relieving himself, unaware that he was being watched.

After Ice shook the last drops of water from his penis, Riley spoke up. "Did you really think you could get away with stealing from us?" he asked Ice. Ice spun around at the sound of Riley's voice. He was so high he never heard him enter.

Squinting at him, Ice tucked himself back inside his jeans and zipped up. "Da fuck you doing here?" he asked a stoic but wound up Riley.

"I'm here to settle some scores, new and old." Riley punctuated his answer with a punch to Ice's face, dislodging several teeth in the process. Before he had time to react, Riley shoved him into the wall before leading him out back to the alley.

***

Ice realized too late that he had made a grave mistake. His plan seemed bullet proof at the time, but now…He wasn't as smart as he thought he was. He hadn't figured Officer Psycho into his game plan.

Riley and his crew had no real dog in his fight against the bosses. Sure they did his uncle's bidding, but that was by rumored reputation only. Whenever heads were knocked or citizens were taken down for nefarious reasons, it was just assumed it was for Craven Wallace at the orders of the Chief. His threat of exposure couldn't touch the rogue cops and Riley knew it. Ice had made the mistake of not securing evidence against the hired muscle, not to mention Riley's personal vendetta against him. He learned too late that Riley Phillips was all about self preservation, not loyalty. And he didn't give a rat's ass about the boss' woes.

Ice swallowed with regret. By now his boy Kane knew he was missing, and hopefully putting his plan into motion. He may not be able to take Riley down, but the satisfaction of taking down his uncle and the mayor was almost worth dying for.

Ice looked around the room at the harden faces of the other men, before squinting up from his prone position on the floor at Riley; this time through swollen eyes. The crazed maniac had been torturing him for the better part of an hour; cutting away pieces of him; mutilating him. Although he was in great pain, Ice refused to give the evil bastard the satisfaction of crying out. He would grind his teeth to nubs before he let that happen.

Now lightheaded and coughing up blood, Ice knew he was close to death. There was no way to stop it. The man had it in for him ever since the death of his beloved Nadia. He coughed some more, wishing he had the strength to laugh. While Nadia was cozying up to Riley, playing the role of the perfect fiancé, she was blowing him on the regular. Yes, Riley would kill him. But he found satisfaction in knowing that alongside the evidence against his uncle, were photos of Nadia on her knees with his dick in her mouth. He just wished he could be around to see the look on the bastard's face when he saw them.

***

Riley bent on one knee to wash his bloodied hands in the river. He was on a high. He gained great satisfaction in killing Ice. He grinned at the fool's failed attempt to stop him; spouting on and on about having proof that Wallace and Allen murdered someone. He gained the greatest pleasure when Ice realized his plan had fallen on deaf ears. Why should he care if he had evidence on the bosses? That was no concern of his. That was their problem.

"What are we going to do about this so-called evidence?" Teddy asked him. He and the others just stood around and watched, while Riley took out his vengeance on the man. That didn't worry him. The evidence against the Chief and the mayor did.

Coming to his feet, Riley shrugged. "Nothing."

"Nothing? You're not going to tell them?" Teddy was incredulous.

Riley, having dried his hands on his pants legs, turned to face him. "Why should we? Just think a minute

Teddy. If those two go down, we can take up where they left off without anyone being the wiser. Unlike them, there is no trail of any kind leading back to us. We're just the hired help, grunts. They don't even see us as equals, considering the fact we handle all the important stuff. I don't know about you, but I'm tired of this measly pay. That bastard Wallace is making millions, while we clear a few thousand here and there. It's about time we got some real money."

Riley thought about blackmailing them himself, but that would only get him so far. And knowing Craven Wallace, he would gladly put a bullet in the back of his head without missing a beat. No, he had to play this smart. When the time was right, he would just point the proper authorities in the right direction and sit back and watch the fireworks. But first, he had to make sure Ice wasn't just blowing smoke up his ass about this so-called evidence. As soon as he could, he planned to take a look inside that safe of his himself, just to make sure there wasn't anything against him there.

He didn't trust Ice. There was something off about him, especially towards the end. He had to admit, the little bastard surprised him. After he realized he wasn't interested in his evidence, he took the torture like a man; no begging or pleading for his life. The bastard even had the nerve to smile as he took his last breath, as if he knew something he didn't. If he was going to take down Allen and Wallace, he didn't need any nasty surprises to come back and bite him in the ass.

"Is everything cleaned up and the body wrapped?" Teddy nodded. "Come on, let's finish this."

Chapter 16

"I want that son of a bitch out of my house now!"

It had been three days since she held her husband and his mistress at gunpoint and Lynette couldn't believe Tony had the nerve to continue to live in their home. He cheated and now he wouldn't leave. It was enough he had backed her into a corner, preventing her from filing for divorce until after the election, but he wanted to remain in the house until then as well. She wanted to be rid of him immediately, but hatefully she found herself under his thumb. The bastard had placed money, from God knows where, in an account setup in her name; money he said was illegally obtained; money that could ruin her if ever discovered. He promised to close the account the moment he won the election which was less than two weeks away.

Lynette couldn't believe she never knew the man she called her husband. The man she thought she married never really existed. After she confronted him about the money, he turned the tables on her; making her an accomplice to his crimes; crimes he said could land them both in prison. She was trapped. She couldn't tell anyone, not even Brody. Tony made sure of that. Any knowledge of his activities by anyone, and he would pull the plug on them both. Lynette really didn't think he would throw himself to the wolves just to get back at her, but she couldn't take that chance. She had built a solid reputation for herself and she wasn't about to lose everything, because of her asshole of a husband.

Brody watched an agitated Lynette pace the room. He felt her pain, but knew how ruthless his brother could be when backed into a corner. He wasn't about to let something as small as infidelity ruin his plans. Tony meant to have that election in his pocket no matter who he had to step on to get it. Knowing his brother, he probably threatened to go to the police over their 'little spat' if she insisted he leave. If she could just hold out for a few more days, she would be free of Tony for good.

He sighed. He hated seeing her like this. She didn't deserve this. It was time he and Tony had a man to man talk about his actions. He had done enough damage to his wife; it was time he let her go. After learning his brother planned to stay until after the election, he came by to talk some sense into him, only to find Lynette alone. Instead of leaving to find his brother, Brody decided to stay to help

Lynette calm down. He knew she needed someone to lean on and he wanted to be that person.

"Lynette, it's just a few more days and then he's gone, out of your life for good." He knew this was killing her. He wanted to take her into his arms and comfort her, but knew he wouldn't want to stop there. He wanted more. He was afraid if he touched her, he would try to take her. Brody knew he had to make her see him before that could happen.

Lynette heard what Brody was saying, but she didn't know if she could take any more of her sadistic husband. Even though he was basically blackmailing her, he had the nerve to try to seduce her; telling her that they should make the best of the situation until he officially moved out. This had enraged her. She couldn't believe the arrogance of the man. She should have killed him when she had the chance.

Still seething, she continued pacing around the room; trying to wrestle her emotions under some sort of control. There was one thing to be grateful for. Tony had the good sense to leave after coming short of forcing himself on her. He had laughed at her agitation; informing her that he would be spending the night out. He even made a crack about her not waiting up. Since uncovering his infidelity, Tony made it a point to rub her face in his affair. He didn't even try to hide where he was headed. This only added fuel to the fire.

Not able to stand anymore, Lynette stopped pacing long enough to grab her keys and head towards the door. "Look Brody, I appreciate what you're saying and for all your help, but I need to get out of here for awhile. I need some air. Can you let yourself out?" Brody nodded.

***

Tony Grimes was on top of the world. Not only had he effectively shut Lynette down, he managed to keep up appearances by staying in the house as well. When she tried making him leave, he lied and said he had implicated her in his illegal activities. He knew how much she valued her reputation and would do anything to protect it. He could thank his mother in-law for that one. Barbara had drilled it into her children's head that reputation was everything.

Tony laughed at the repulsive look Lynette gave him. She didn't have to worry about him touching her. He had no intentions of ever sleeping with her again. He just wanted to torment her before leaving to see Cassie. His informing his wife where he was headed had been the icing on the evening. He didn't even try to hide the fact he was still sleeping with Cassie. Why should he? He didn't have to pretend anymore and he was glad. Playing the loving, dutiful husband had gotten old and boring ages ago. Lynette was an intelligent and beautiful woman, but not *enough* woman for him. She was too prim and proper. Whereas she served a purpose for him in the public eye, she sucked behind closed doors. She had too many boundaries that were archaic and in his opinion deal breakers when it came to the bedroom. If he hadn't needed her, he would have dumped her years ago. Hell he wouldn't have married her.

But Cassie, his sweet uninhibited Cassie, satisfied every inch of him. He got hard just thinking of the ways Cassie kept him satisfied. It hadn't taken much to smooth things over with her. He just promised her more of the same and she fell for it as usual. Women could be so stupid. Tony shook his head in amused wonder. Yes, he was still on top of his game. He had all of his women in line and under his control.

Pulling into his favorite parking spot in Cassie's complex, Tony got out of the car. He checked his watch;

noting he was over an hour late. He wasn't worried. Usually she would have had a fit when he arrived late, but after he promised to marry her, Cassie became more lenient; especially now that Lynette was on board with the situation. Cassie knew she had him all to herself—at least for now anyway. Things were about to come to a close for her, she just didn't know it. He already had her replacement lined up and would be making the transition right after he won the election. Like Lynette, Cassie had served her purpose. It was time to put both women behind him.

Bending to catch a glimpse of himself in the side view mirror, Tony Grimes didn't notice the person standing behind him. As he straightened, he caught a shadow before he was hit over the head and dragged from his favorite parking spot.

***

Cassie Duvall stood on the dock, looking out at the river. This was her favorite place when times got rough. The soothing sluicing of the water against the shore always helped to clear her thoughts; making it possible for her to make the right decisions.

She had made some hard choices over the last few days, but she felt they were the right choices. It was beyond time to cut ties to Tony. Deep down, she knew when she hooked up with him it would end this way. But she couldn't stop herself from getting involved with him. He was like an addicting drug that she couldn't say no to until now. Men like Tony Grimes were what her mama said were no earthly good. Her mama was right and she should have listened.

Tony had disappointed her many times before and Lynette threatening to kill them should have been the last straw; but it wasn't. Up until yesterday, she still had some small misguided faith that he would make good on his promises. She still believed he would marry her after the election was over. But reality came after overhearing him ordering flowers for another woman when he thought she was in the shower. The same array of flowers he used to send to her. And just like that, he was replacing her. But the joke was on him, she got rid of him first.

Taking the coveted object from her jacket pocket, she flung it into the river. She listened as it made a plopping sound as it broke the water's surface. Finally she was free of Tony Grimes.

Chapter 17

Father Mason Coburn chewed his Porterhouse steak in ecstasy. After accepting the priesthood, he never thought he could eat so well. He took a sip from his glass of expensive Bordeaux to wash down the perfectly aged and seasoned meat. The cook had out done herself tonight, he thought, as he cut another piece of his steak.

Father Coburn, once the revered priest of his community, now considered himself the personal spiritual advisor to Metro City's mayor *and* to the Dog Street Mob. He gave advice and kept secret their dirty deeds, all in the name of the Lord. And in return for these services, along with their joint business ventures, he lived the high life.

It all began innocent enough. He would hear their confessions and absolved them of their sins. As his popularity grew, so did his finances. Along with the confessions came money. Each week after Mass, someone would leave large amounts of cash in the bottom drawer of his bureau in his modest room at the rectory. He never saw or guessed the person who put the envelopes there; only that the money came. At first he tried to find the owner to return it, but whenever he inquired of its source, he was met with silence. Soon he stopped inquiring and kept it hidden away until he could find use for it.

It didn't take him long to find use for it. In the beginning, he anonymously placed some of the cash into the collection box, but later he thought better of it. He eased his conscience by claiming God didn't want tainted money and began lavishing himself with food, wine and his favorite vice—women.

Father Coburn never agreed with the Church's stance on banning sexuality for its clergy. He loved women and always had. While some of his fellow priests indulged in the forbidden fruit of young children, Coburn turned his eyes toward prostitutes and the occasional willing parishioner. But when his former charge, Craven Wallace, discovered his vice, he made him a proposition he couldn't refuse—his very own membership in the mayor's family of business partners.

Coburn tried his hand at being the good parish priest; watching over his flock; comforting the grieving and advising the godly. But he soon found there was no joy in it. The more he comforted the less fortunate, the bigger the emptiness grew inside of him. Sure he turned some of the neighborhood bullies and thieves around, but it hadn't been enough for him. He required more. He required power.

His greatest and most lucrative accomplishment had been the reforming of two of the toughest thugs he had ever encountered; the current mayor and chief of police of their fair city. And after they were well established in their positions, they helped him to see the light. They helped him realize he could have more than what the Church had to offer. They offered him power and wealth. And without a backwards glance he took it.

Father Coburn paused at the slight tap at his door. His eyes glanced up at the clock to see it was a little before seven. He smirked. She was early. He hadn't expected his guess until later. Wiping his mouth with his expensive hand embroidered napkin, he told his guest to enter.

The woman quickly slipped into the Father's quarters, hoping not to be seen by anyone who may be wandering the hallway. She told herself she would stand up to him and make this the last time, but knew if he demanded it, she would be returning again. The Father had laughed when she told him she wouldn't be back. He knew she would come back. So when she texted him to say she was on her way, she could imagine the smirk displayed on his handsome face. The smirk he now wore right.

Without a word, Father Coburn stood and gestured for her. He would have to make this quick. He didn't want his food to get cold. Besides, he didn't really want her. He just needed to remind her of her place; to keep her in line. He took great pleasure in the game he played with her. In the beginning, she foolishly thought she was in control, only to quickly learn she had been the prey all along. She thought tonight would be her final turn with his friends, but she was sadly mistaken. He would release her when it was convenient for him, not her.

Reluctantly, the woman forced herself to walk across the room, before falling to her knees before him. The good Father was already naked from the waist down, anticipating her arrival.

***

Father Coburn rolled off his favorite with a still erect penis. He couldn't get enough of her. The more he bedded her, the more excited he became. He marveled at how she never complained no matter what he asked of her. She was his rarest of finds and on some level he thought he loved her. She wasn't like the others he played with; she was different; special even. He often wondered if it was because she always came to him willingly, without any fuss or coercion. Unlike the others, if threats weren't involved the others would never return.

Even though he had never outwardly threatened her, he would never let her go. She was his for as long as he liked, whether she understood this or not. He let her play her little game of wanting to break ties with him, but if she ever seriously sought to leave him, he would make sure she paid and paid dearly.

Wanting more of his rare and delicate bird, he rolled back on top of her and entered her again

Chapter 18

Chief Warren Allen left a message on his wife's cell phone. He would be late coming home tonight. He briefly wondered why she wasn't picking up. He had tried their home number and reached voicemail there too.

Warren shrugged. Sadie was probably out doing more of her charity work. Ever since she got involved with the church's literacy program, it had demanded more of her time. He guessed she may have been a little bored after he persuaded her to stop teaching. She had balked at first, but he was in a position to spoil his wife and he meant to do just that. So now when she wasn't helping others, she was pampering herself at the spa or running off to New York to do some shopping. It was his pleasure to provide her with those luxuries. She deserved it.

Sadie was the love of his life and always would be. The woman was amazing, sticking with him through those times of him running and ruling the streets; never knowing if he would live or die. She always wanted better for him and pushed him to attend college and earn a degree. When he chose to forgo college in order to join the police force, she was disappointed, but supported him just the same.

Sadie mostly wanted him out of the gang and into something more respectable. And he couldn't have honored that desire more than becoming Metro City's newest top cop, making his wife more proud of him than he thought he deserved. So because she selflessly stood with him through thick and thin, he made sure she wanted for nothing.

Warren tried her phone again only to get voicemail again. It was just as well. Since he and Craven expanded their operations to include gun running, he had been working overtime to get the shipments to their perspective buyers on time. He thought they were doing quite well with just the drugs until the money started pouring in. And when Coburn added his little vice to the mix, it increased their income a hundred fold; netting them millions a month in revenue.

He shook his head at it all. He and Craven had started out together as teens running drugs for the OG's back in the day. And many years later, they were calling their own shots and had moved up to become the kings on top of the pile. They had come a long way in a short period of time. They now had more money than they knew what to do with. After Craven was re-elected, he was going to take his wife anywhere in the world she wanted to go, first class all the way. They both deserved it.

Listening to the creaking of the crates being pried open and nailed shut again, Chief Allen watched his men, as they went through and counted each gun and crate to make sure none were missing. He had learned the hard way about trust. He made the mistake in trusting one of his drug dealers to handle the shipments unsupervised, only to have the man steal from them. The idiot had made a bigger mistake by setting up a deal with buyers there in town, which would surely bring down the wrath of the ATF and the FBI if discovered.

Through a tip from one of his more loyal employees, he was able to stop the man and collect all of the guns, before he had a chance to sell them. He remembered that night clearly. They had been right there in the warehouse. Craven was furious, wanting to kill the dealer himself, something that could never happen. He understood Craven's rage, but just one misstep and they all could end up behind bars. He couldn't allow his friend to get his hands dirty. Craven was a natural leader and should remain so. He simply did what had to be done. Taking care of difficult issues is why Craven hired him. Without hesitation, he took the dealer out; sending a clear message to anyone else who thought to cross them.

Nothing had changed; it was just like the old days. Whenever trouble came around, he took care of it. No matter how big or how small, he always had a solution to the problem. And that was his natural talent. It was what made him the perfect candidate for Police Chief. He had Father Coburn to thank for that. If he hadn't stepped in each time he was accused of a crime, he would have been behind bars instead of overseeing them.

After watching the last crate being loaded onto the truck, Chief Allen checked his watch. It was still early. Rolling his neck from side to side, he decided he would make a stop before he headed home. He was still tense from losing money due to his nephew's foolishness. But now that the problem had been solved, he wanted to relax a little. He loved his wife, but wasn't beyond sampling some of Coburn's product from time to time. Besides, she wasn't expecting him anytime soon.

***

Sadie Allen trembled as she let herself into the home she shared with her police chief husband. She walked on unsteady legs to the console to the security system. The blaring beeping wasn't helping her mood. Her hands trembled violently as she keyed in the appropriate numbers; stopping the offending noise.

Switching on a lamp light, she sighed with gratitude that Warren hadn't made it home. She checked her watch and discovered she had better than two hours before he was due in for the night. Moving towards their bedroom, Sadie pulled her expensive heels from her grateful feet. She had to walk around in those ridiculous things for several hours, trying to please her 'date' of the evening. She wanted to cry, but didn't dare. Her eyes would be too puffy to explain away and there was no way her husband or anyone else could find out she was on the hoe stroll; the upper crust of strolls, but the hoe stroll just the same.

It all started when she made the brutal mistake of sleeping with Father Coburn. The man was handsome, so she found flirting with him easy. The flirting started when she volunteered to tutor some of the parish's young adults in the church's literacy program. He would often join her to help set up for her class. She found the work rewarding after leaving her job as a teacher, to become a pampered housewife. But Sadie soon craved excitement she couldn't find in being a mere housewife or volunteer; excitement she found one evening in Father Coburn's bed.

She thought their trysts were all fun and games until she tried to end it. That's when Coburn put his collar aside and the devil showed up in its place. He agreed to let her go, under one condition—she had to service a couple of his friends. She would never forget the cold calculating mask that transformed his handsome face. Until that moment, she thought he was joking. That was the moment she realized her mistake. He had set her up. She soon discovered she was only one of several women he had under his thumb; all lonely well to do women who had everything to lose if discovered. The couple of friends turned into twelve which he jokingly referred to as the twelve disciples; prominent men who were movers and shakers of the community. Some were even acquaintances of her husband.

Sadie hobbled to the master suite to draw a scalding bath. She didn't care if the hot water took her skin from her bones. Her appointment of the night had been beyond anything she could have imagined. The man, after making her parade around in those whorish shoes, took her in every opening he could shove his dick into. He even rubbed the tip of it across her nose and into both of her ears. It was bad enough she had to endure that disgusting pig, but she had been summoned to Coburn's quarters before meeting with the man. He claimed he missed her, when in reality he wanted to humiliate her some more. She was beyond disgusted.

Even though the good Father assured her it would be her last job, she didn't believe him. Knowing how disgusting the man was, he told her he saved the best for last. And even though she hoped she was wrong, she wouldn't bank on it. She brought in too much money; money she never saw a dime of. She was Coburn's for free hire and all because she wanted to walk on the wild side by sleeping with a priest.

After starting the bath with a ton of bath salts, Sadie searched through the bottles on the bathroom vanity, until she found what she was looking for. She picked up the bottle with the blue liquid and turned it up. She used the mouthwash to cleanse away the awful taste of the man on her tongue. She nearly gagged thinking about the things he made her do. Swishing the liquid around a few more times, she spat it from her mouth into the sink. Now she could have that bottle of wine she so desperately needed.

Chapter 19

"Breaking news! Another body has been found floating in Belle River. The authorities haven't released the identity, other than it appears to be the body of a white male. This is the fourth body found floating in the river within the last six months. The bodies…"

Kobe dismissed the video on his iPad with a tap. It was the third news report he'd watched that morning. Mildly perplexed, he scrolled through the search results hoping for more information. It looked like the police department had a serial killer on its hands. It wasn't the number of bodies found that intrigued him, but how they were killed. Each had been mutilated with what the coroner stated was an oddly serrated blade, and up until now, the victims had all been women. He had the nagging feeling that he was missing something; something important.

While he sat in Hudson's Investigations' conference room he tried to determine what was so important about the details of the killings. He had been summoned to the office for a meeting with KT, Brody and Tor. He was still racking his brain on what he was missing, when the trio entered the room. Putting aside his tablet and his misgivings about the bodies, he stood to greet them.

"Good to see you again Kobe." Tor shook his outstretched hand.

"You too…KT, Brody." He nodded at the others as they took their seats.

"So, bring me up to date on what you guys have," Tor addressed the group. He had been working on another case and it was his first chance to get up to speed on their progress. "Oh, before you began, great work on handling that situation at Tony's. I'm glad to hear no one got hurt and it was resolved peacefully. But I am concerned that the police weren't called."

Brody cleared his throat on this. "That was my call. Lynette was angry, but not angry enough to really hurt anyone. She said she just wanted to scare them nothing more. And since no one was hurt, I didn't see the need in dragging the police into it. Besides, I have her gun." Brody felt that was the end of it. Although he worried about Lynette, he didn't think she was dangerous. She seemed to have settled down some when he talked to her earlier that morning. She said Tony hadn't bothered to come home, which was a relief for them both.

Tor studied Brody a moment before nodding his approval. "KT what do we have?"

"Kobe and I have finalized a list of all the players, at least we hope we didn't over look anyone. But with all of the data we've collected, it mainly involves the mayor, chief of police, a few of the police officers, Councilman Hayes, and…" She trailed off after Hayes' name; letting her eyes drift in Brody's direction. She had kept this under wraps until now, but she had no other choice but to reveal the last piece of the puzzle. "I'm sorry Brody. Your brother is up to his neck in this mess."

All eyes fell on Brody. He was shocked to say the least. "What do you mean Tony's involved?" He wasn't asking so much because of Tony, but because of Lynette. Had he involved her in his mess?

Kobe spoke up. "Your brother is the one who's arranged for software to be used to rig the voting machines. We have phone calls and text messages that place him in the middle of this thing." Kobe checked his notes. "The software was ordered through a startup company that doesn't seem to exist on paper. We don't know who the contact person is, but it should be in his hot little hands tomorrow. According to the information we've gathered, the delivery is set for tomorrow afternoon." He and KT had been working overtime to crack this case and it seemed it would be over once they catch Tony with the goods.

KT squeezed Brody's hand. Brody always said his brother was a bastard, but she didn't think he knew how much of one until today. He was about to ask if Lynette was involved when Detective Eric Valero tapped on the open door.

"Good morning everyone," Detective Valero greeted the group, before leaning down to kiss KT on the month. Kobe raised an eyebrow at this gesture.

"Kobe, I don't think you've met Detective Valero have you?" Tor asked.

"No we haven't met." Kobe rose to shake the man's hand.

"Good to finally meet. Kaitlin has told me much about you. She says you're a good PI even if you don't work for Tor." Eric smiled at Kobe before giving a wink to KT. KT shook her head at his antics.

Kaitlin. He called her Kaitlin. It appears she has exceptions about her name after all, Kobe thought.

He only nodded before retaking his seat. It seemed the detective knew all about him but KT failed to mention anything about her friend, professional or otherwise. He looked across the table at her and saw a radiance he'd never seen before. Although he'd come to witness her rough edges, this man brought out the softness in her; a softness he wouldn't have suspected she possessed. Frowning on this, KT's interaction with Valero suddenly disturbed him, and he didn't know why. Especially since the disturbance he felt was akin to jealousy. Before he could ponder more on this unexpected sensation, Kobe shut it down. It was a feeling he didn't want to pursue.

"So what brings you here detective?" Tor asked.

"I know from Kaitlin that you're investigating Tony Grimes…and there is no good way to say this but…" he turned towards Brody. "The body we fished out of the river this morning was Tony's. I'm sorry man." Once again, all eyes were on Brody.

***

Brody sat silently as the news of his brother's death ricocheted around the room. His brother was dead. Brody felt hollow inside; lifeless. He only heard bits and pieces of the conversation around him. Everyone in the room had faded into the background. Brody had questions. Starting with: Did the police have any clues as to what happened to him? He didn't have to wait long before he had the answer.

Although Tony was dumped in the river as the others had been, the police believed he wasn't killed by the same assailant as the others. Whereas the other victims were mutilated, Tony had been stabbed several times in the back with a smooth edged blade. It was also believed that his murder was a crime of passion and not the mayhem of a serial killer.

When Valero mentioned this, Brody's mind refocused. His head was spinning with the possibility.

"Brody? Brody?" Tor was calling his name.

"Yes.." he was trying to wrap his mind around it all.

"Do you know where Lynette was last night?" Tor was beginning to rethink his approval of Brody not contacting the police. He studied him. From the look on Brody's face, he thought Lynette maybe involved too.

At the mention of Lynette's name, Brody's demeanor changed. *Lynette didn't do this. Why are they asking about Lynette?* Brody shook his head. He may not have known where Lynette ran off to, but he knew she didn't do it and he resented the fact that everyone in the room thought she had.

He closed his eyes and thought back on the previous night. After Lynette left, he had gone into her bedroom where he found her lingerie drawer. He entertained himself by rubbing a pair of her lacy panties across his face; wishing he was inside her. After replacing the panties, he let himself out.

Eric's gaze shifted from Tor to Brody and back again. "Is there something I should know? He asked the group.

KT sighed. "There was an incident at the Grimes' a few days ago. Lynette Grimes came home to find her husband in bed with another woman. She confronted them with a gun." KT knew she would hear about this later, but Eric had to understand, she wasn't obligated to share every aspect of her job with him.

"What happened?" Eric asked her.

While KT gave Eric the blow by blow account, Kobe studied Brody. He was understandably upset, but had become more so after Lynette's name was mentioned. He wondered what Brody was hiding. Did he think she killed his brother or was there something else going on? Whatever it was, Kobe didn't like it. In his opinion, Brody was being too protective of his sister in-law.

When KT finished up, Tor made a mental note not to let this happen again. From that point on, any incident that involved gunplay or any other life threatening matter would be reported to the police immediately. Even if Lynette Grimes didn't kill her husband, it still looked bad. He had a great working relationship with MCPD and he wanted to keep it that way.

Eric wrote down some details. "I will be dropping in on Mrs. Grimes when I leave here."

"Does she know her husband is dead?" Kobe asked; still eyeing Brody. Everyone was asking the questions he should have been asking.

Eric nodded. "Another detective was dispatched to inform her." Eric nodded at everyone, before leaving to continue his investigation.

"Lynette didn't kill Tony. She couldn't have. If she was going to kill him, don't you think she would have done so when she caught him in her bed with Cassie?" Brody placed his face in his palms. He couldn't believe they suspected Lynette.

Yes, he was way too concerned with his sister in-law. Where was the compassion for his brother? Kobe wanted to know. Maybe Lynette did kill her husband and Brody knows it.

Chapter 20

Big Ed's hands hadn't stopped trembling since hearing the news that a white male had been pulled from the river. He was certain it was his son. The police were no closer to finding Carrington than they were a week ago. Even after learning it was Grimes' body found, he still couldn't stop shaking.

"Here drink this." Craven handed him a three finger glass of whiskey. It was early, but not nearly early enough not to want a drink. He, Ed and Warren Allen were meeting in the mayor's office. They had just learned of Tony Grimes death.

Allen took a healthy swallow from his glass. "What are we going to do now. Grimes was our only connection to our problem and now that he's dead…" He trailed off. He wanted to kick himself for suggesting that Grimes should handle the software transaction solely. But they wanted to distance themselves in case he got caught. Now they had no way of getting the software needed to ensure the election.

Craven refilled his glass before pacing his office. What were they going to do? The election was in a few days and they didn't have time to seek out a new contact. "Do you think his wife has any information?"

Warren chuckled. "You know as well as I do, he didn't like her, let alone trust her with that kind of information. But he may have left some sort of details at his home. We've been through his office and found nothing. That dizzy secretary of his was so out of it about his death she didn't care what we did with his personal papers. I had my men go over everything with a fine tooth comb…nothing!"

"One thing is for sure, if there is something to find, we need to get to it before your detectives do." Big Ed had gotten himself under control enough to add to their worry. On top of everything else he had no intentions of going to prison.

Chief Allen nodded. Picking up the phone he called Phillips. "I need you to do something for me."

***

Tony was dead. Brenda Sims bent to pick up some of the papers that had been thrown about the floor in her boss's office. She thought the police would have been more respectful of one of their own. What they were looking for, she knew they hadn't found it. She had only been Tony Grimes assistant a short time, but she knew where all of the bodies were buried so to speak. And one thing was for sure, they weren't all in his office. She knew the moment they arrived they weren't looking for any clues to who may have killed him. Not one time had they asked about any death threats or mishaps concerning her boss. In fact they dismissed her all together.

Brenda wiped away a single tear. That was all she would allow herself to display. There wasn't time to show any real emotion. She had bigger things to worry about. Now that Tony was dead, what should she do next?

Chapter 21

Cassie Duvall sat in the interrogation room staring back at Detective Valero. After all she had been through with Tony, she now found herself a suspect in his murder. After learning he was dead, she knew she should have felt something but she didn't. Not one tear had fallen, not one; and she wasn't sorry about it.

Had she been angry with Tony? Sure. She was angry when he threw her under the bus when his crazy wife held a gun on them. And yes, she was especially angry when she discovered he was about to dump her. And yes, she may have been angry enough to kill him, but she hadn't. She had made her peace once she tossed his so-called engagement ring into Belle River. And yes she had been angry about the ring. It was only after she discovered the five carat diamond setting wasn't real, did she realize it was more of an appeasement ring to keep her hanging on, until he was finished with her.

She remembered the hope she felt when he placed it on her finger. It was just hours after the incident with his wife. He had shown up at her place all apologetic; telling her how much he loved her and wanted her to be his wife.

Tony even got down on one knee to propose. And like a fool she believed he was sincere. She was so happy she almost knocked him over when she leaped into his arms to accept. But that was before she heard him ordering those damn flowers for another woman. She should have known better than to get involved with a married man.

When Cassie met Tony he was all sweet and attentive, unlike any of the men she usually dated. They met in a coffee shop one morning when she was on her way to work. Some rude customer had knocked her coffee to the ground and hadn't even bothered to stop walking let alone apologize. The man was too engrossed in his important phone conversation to care. Tony, being the gentleman he was, helped her clean up and bought her another latte. It was on from there.

They started meeting casually at first, for lunch, sometimes an early dinner when Lynette was out of town visiting her family. Tony made it known from the beginning that he was married and made no excuses for it. He told Cassie he liked her company and didn't see why they couldn't become good friends. She readily agreed. After her last involvement she wasn't interested in a relationship, so she was all for something strictly platonic.

This arrangement worked perfectly for Cassie until she found herself strained in a Denver hotel during a snow storm. They ran into each other in the lobby. She was coming from one of the many conferences she'd attended that week and he was there interviewing a witness for a trial. By the time they encountered each other, they both were in need of a good dinner and a few glasses of wine. They had a wonderful dinner together, and a couple of bottles of wine. With the snow coming down outside, and the candle light at dinner, Cassie let her guard down. Seeing Tony had been a nice surprise.

At the end of dinner, Tony offered to accompany her to her room. But once her door was opened, instead of saying goodnight and leaving it at that, he pulled her to him; kissing her feverishly; all the while backing her deeper into her room. Once inside, he closed the door with is foot, never taking his lips or hands from her body. He had stripped her naked before she knew what hit her. To this day she still didn't remember when or how he had gotten out of his clothes.

From there he back walked her to the bed. Her back had barely touched the mattress before he was on top of her, whispering to her how good they would be together.

Before Tony entered her, he straddled her upper body to where she could get an up close and personal acquaintance with his erection. He arrogantly wanted her to know what she was in for. He was impressive and he knew it. He boldly stroked himself, as he explained what he was going to do with it.

After he was confident that he had her full attention, he maneuvered himself between her thighs, leveraging her bottom on a pillow then drove hard inside her. Cassie had been in heaven. Not only did the man boast a big stick he knew how to use it.

Cassie almost smiled from that memory, until she remembered she was sitting in a police station.

Chapter 22

Eric Valero stood between two interrogation rooms; shifting his gaze between the two suspects. In one room was Lynette Grimes, wife of Assistant District Attorney Tony Grimes. In the other sat his mistress, Cassie Duvall. Both women had motive to kill Tony, and neither had a clear alibi, as to their whereabouts when he was killed. He didn't know what to think.

Tony Grimes' car was found parked near Cassie's condo. After learning of the incident that took place at the Grimes' home, he paid Cassie a visit. He assumed she would be pretty upset with Grimes after being held at gunpoint by his wife. Not to mention, he chose to stay with Lynette after the incident. And after learning of the proposal and her discovery of yet another woman, Eric found her to be more than a viable suspect, which led him to request her presence downtown for a more formal questioning.

She said she had been expecting Tony, but at the last minute decided not to see him. Cassie told him, she left home before Tony arrived to clear her head. She was ending the relationship, but needed time to distance herself emotionally before seeing him. She claimed she left him a note taped to her door; stating she would see him the next day. She said when she returned home, the note was gone so assumed he got the message and left. When he asked where she'd gone that night, he discovered she had been down by the river. And since Tony was fished from the river…well, she immediately became a top suspect.

Now it was time to talk to the wife who had every reason in the world to want her husband dead. Picking up a folder, he headed into the interrogation room.

He knocked on the door for the officer to allow him entrance. "Mrs. Grimes, I'm sorry to keep you waiting." Eric entered the room to a stoic Lynette.

Lynette smoothed back her hair. She was tired and sure she looked a mess. The stress of everything had begun to take its toll on her.

"Can I get you anything…water, soda? Lynette shook her head. She just wanted this over with.

"Alright, let's get to it then. Could you tell me about the night your husband was killed? Where were you, what you doing?" Eric watched her closely. She looked tired; worn; as if all the fight had left her.

"As I've stated before, I was out driving around, nothing more."

"Did you see anyone? Talk to anyone?"

"Listen detective. I didn't kill my husband. If I was going to kill him, I would have done so when I found him with that...that woman." Lynette dismissed this with a fling of a hand. She almost wished she had killed him; at least she would have been sitting there for reason, instead of having her time wasted.

"Your brother in-law stated you were agitated when you left the house that night. Can you tell me why." Eric already knew the answer, but he wanted to hear it from her. He still couldn't understand how Grimes had persuaded her to let him stay in the house, after discovering his affair. The woman had gone as far as to pull a gun on him, yet she allowed him to remain in the house.

"Tony wouldn't move out and I wanted him gone. That's why I was agitated." The mere thought of Tony having something over her galled her. This thought brought back to mind the threat he'd made; the exposure of money in an account that bore her name. All the color drained from her face. Would the police find the money and assume she was in on Tony's schemes? Maybe she should get a lawyer. She couldn't go to prison for something her no good husband did.

"You know, I've changed my mind. I would like an attorney." Lynette eyed the detective with contempt. She knew how this worked. She had heard enough stories from Tony to know this could get ugly very quickly, if she didn't stop it now. Besides, she couldn't tell him where she really was. No one could ever know.

Eric saw the immediate change in Lynette and wondered what nerve had he touched. Whatever it was, he believed it was tied into why he remained at the house, despite the fact she hadn't wanted him there.

"Sure, but you're not under arrest. We're just talking here." There wasn't anything he could hold her for. They had no evidence that she committed a crime.

"Am I free to go?" Lynette stood, gathering her things. Eric gestured towards the door. Lynette hurriedly left the room.

Eric sighed. She was hiding something. Could she have killed her husband? At that moment there was a knock at the door. One of the officers stuck her head in.

"Ms. Duvall's alibi checks out. A night fisherman saw her on the docks. He said she was there for a couple of hours just staring into the water. From there she sat in her car awhile, before she finally left." The officer shrugged before leaving him to his thoughts.

He would have to question the fisherman. But if the man was a stranger, he didn't have a reason to lie. That only left one other person who had motive to murder Tony Grimes, his wife.

***

Lynette sat in her car with her arms wrapped around her torso. "How the hell did I get in this mess? Tony cheats, gets himself killed, and I end up with one foot in jail." She sighed. She couldn't tell anyone where she was that night. Even if she could, she didn't think Mason would back her up. He had too much to lose. And in spite of everything she was beginning to think she loved him and didn't want to see him hurt in anyway. It wasn't his fault Tony was dead.

She started the car to head home. Maybe she should call him. Maybe he could help her somehow. She dismissed this. She couldn't call him with her problems. But if the police thought she killed her husband, what was she going to do? Lynette blew out a long sigh. She wanted to go to him now, but she thought better of it. The police could be watching her. She shouldn't have gone there last night, but as always, she couldn't help herself.

Chapter 23

Riley waited thirty minutes before entering Ice's home. He had been watching the house for hours, waiting for his chance to slip inside. Ice's crew had left for the evening to party at some club. Although they assumed Ice was dead, they still held out hope that he would come walking through that door someday.

Getting out of the car, Riley looked up and down the street as he made his way to the back of the house. He had to see for himself if Ice was lying about evidence against Allen and Wallace. And more importantly, did he have any dirt on him. Trying a patio door, he popped the flimsy lock with his pocket knife. He shook his head at how easy it was. People never learned. Riley stuck his head into the room before letting himself inside. He waited to hear any movement that indicated some one was home. Hearing nothing, he stepped inside closing the door behind him.

Using a flashlight he made his way to a bedroom he assumed was Ice's, since it was the most furnished. He opened draws, rifled through papers. He knew what he was looking for wouldn't be found there but he was curious. Finally giving up on finding anything of useful, he moved into the walk-in closet. Pocketing his flashlight he turned on the closet's light. There tucked in a corner stood a waist high safe. Riley dropped to his knees producing a piece of paper from his pocket. On it held the combination to Ice's safe. When the lock disengaged, Riley smiled. Ice had given him the correct numbers.

"So far, so good. Now let's see if you were telling the truth." He opened the door to find a few papers, a small stack of cash, along with a large manila envelope. Riley sat back on his hunches and pulled the envelope from the safe. Expecting to find proof of his boss' dirty dealings, what he found instead enraged him. Contained in the envelope were photos of Nadia, his Nadia, on her knees servicing Ice, along with others displaying her in compromising positions.

Riley felt light headed. How could this be? This was Nadia; his sweet Nadia. How could she have been a part of this. Coming to his feet, Riley staggered from the room, from the house; not bothering to close the safe or turn off the light. He didn't care if they knew someone had been there. Clutching the photos to his chest, he made his way back to his car. He took deep breaths before starting the car and driving away. If Ice wasn't dead, he would kill him all over again.

***

Kane grinned when he returned to find Ice's safe open. He knew Phillips would come. But the grin was short lived. If Phillips had been there, that meant Ice really was dead. He rubbed his fingers across his lips. He would have to tell the crew Ice was indeed gone. Closing the safe, he made a call. Now that Phillips had played his hand, it was time he played his.

***

Riley Phillips was still enraged when he reached his apartment. He wanted to throw something, he wanted to kill! All this time he thought Nadia was innocent. He paced around his living room trying to clear his mind of the images that had been burned there. That bitch was just another skank whore. Picking up the framed photo he had of her on his mantle, he threw it across the room.

"THAT BITCH!" Riley was beside himself. How could he have not known. How! Finally calming down enough to need a drink, he stalked to the kitchen for a beer.

He had swallowed the entire bottle when his phone rang. The call was from a blocked number.

"Hello!"

"I see you found what you were looking for," the caller said.

"Who is this?" Riley put the beer bottle down to focus on the call. What the hell was this about.

"The photos, you have the photos?" The caller asked.

Riley ran a hand down his face. Someone else knew about the photos. "What do you want?" He was in no mood to beat around the bush or play games.

"I have the other information you came for, but it will cost you if you find it important enough to have in your possession. The proof against the good mayor and your chief?"

"How much?"

The caller gave Riley a figure and instructions on how to obtain the information he wanted before hanging up. Riley finished a second bottle of beer before reaching for another.

***

Kane opened a second safe hidden behind Ice's dresser to retrieve the real prize. He knew he was supposed to send it to one of the news stations, but he saw an opportunity to make a few dollars instead. He would sell it to Phillips. He loved his boy Ice, but it was time he got paid. He thought about blackmailing the mayor directly, but quickly squashed that idea. Wallace Craven was one of their own and it was disrespectful to turn on an OG. He would leave that up to Phillips.

***

Riley placed the stash of cash under the wheel well of the car as instructed. Walking around to the other side of the car, he knelt down to search for the envelope he was looking for. It was taped under the wheel well on the driver's side of the beat up car. Not taking the time to inspect his find, he hurried back to his car and drove out of the rundown neighborhood. He didn't stop until he made it back to his place where he pulled more photos from the envelope along with a flash drive with the label murder taped to it. This time the stills were of Wallace and Allen executing one of their junky dealers. Along with the photos was a second smaller drive. Curious, Riley moved to his laptop to have a look. This wasn't part of the deal. He hoped it wasn't more of Nadia with that bastard Ice.

Plugging the drive into the appropriate slot, a video appeared on the screen. A grin spread across Riley's face at what he saw. There was Sadie Allen on all fours being thoroughly and roughly screwed by a man who was not her husband. Surprised, he fast forwarded the video until he came to a clip with Sadie and Councilman Hayes. Riley slowly shook his head in wonder. For an old dude, Hayes was roughing her up pretty good. The video was ten minutes in before he realized it had audio. Pushing the volume up, he learned from the conversation Hayes was having with Sadie, the Chief's wife was selling herself.

Clapping his hands and yelling wildly, Riley didn't know which piece of evidence he liked better; the murder or Sadie Allen whoring. Either way, both men were done in this town and he had the power to make it happen.

***

Kane counted out his money. He hoped Riley enjoyed his bonus, thanks to Father Coburn. The sadistic bastard liked to record all of his girl's escapades. Kane shook his head. He happened upon the videos by mistake. One day when he was dropping off the fathers 'love offering', he found Coburn's laptop open to one of the clips. Not having time to view it, he downloaded it, along with everything else in the folder to a flash drive. He remembered how his eyes had widened when he realized what he had. He could imagine how Phillips was reacting. At the time, he didn't know what to do with it. But once he made the deal with Phillips, he knew.

Kane didn't mind dropping a little extra on Phillips. Ice was his boy and all, but he hated the way he treated women, especially Nadia. The girl didn't deserve that. Ice had always wanted a piece of Nadia, but could never find a way to make that happen. After he found out she was marrying Phillips, he found his opening. He knew Nadia wanted a big flashy wedding but couldn't afford it, so he offered to help her with the expenses; claiming he wanted to see a neighborhood sista do good. But Nadia found out too late that Ice's help came with a price. She had spent nearly fifteen grand, before Ice called in to collect.

Kane's jaw tightened. Yeah, Ice was his boy, but he was glad the sick bastard was dead.

Chapter 24

Brody Grimes blinked as he slid another mutilated body off the pier into the cold water. It was his sixth. When he killed, it was as if he were in a trace; a deep sleep that over took him until his blood lust was satisfied. Washing his hands in the river, he wished he had brought a beer with him. Once the killing was done, he would sit on the edge of the landing; swinging his feet while he enjoyed a calming brew. But tonight he was in a hurry. There wasn't time to stop and pick up a six pack. Kobe and KT were expecting him.

After making sure his hands were clean, he gave his clothes the once over to assure there was not a speck of blood to be seen. Untidiness might escape KT because she worked with him, but he doubted it would escape Kobe. The man seemed to be watching him closely these days and he didn't know why. He was always careful, so there was no reason to suspect he knew anything. But still…

Brody started killing shortly after discovering Tony's affairs. He couldn't believe his brother would cheat on a woman as good as Lynette. But what he really couldn't understand was why Lynette never caught on before the showdown in her bedroom. As much as he loved her, he hated her for being so stupid. How could a woman that intelligent not see something that was right before her eyes? He tried not to think about Lynette in this way. He needed to always keep her in a loving manner. Because when he didn't, things got bad; really bad.

His first kill was by mistake. He was having lunch at his favorite diner when he saw his brother coming out of a low-rent hotel with a blond. He wasn't sure what was going on, until Tony leaned in to kiss the woman. Then he knew Tony was up to his old tricks again. Tony had been playing around right up to the night before his wedding; promising Brody it would all end the moment he spoke his wedding vows. Brody had taken him at his word until that day. He knew then Tony had never stopped.

Brody watched his brother plow through several women before the pressure that resided in him couldn't be held. It all came to a head, after he worked a case gathering information on a cheating husband. He had taken several photos of the man in various compromising positions that would surly lead to the demise of his marriage. But when he met with the wife to deliver the evidence, the woman wasn't even outraged. She cried a few tears while vowing to forgive the cheating bastard. Feeling an urge he couldn't explain, Brody rushed the woman stabbing and slicing her face until she was unrecognizable. After his handy work was completed, he calmly shoved her off the pier into the water. Realizing he needed to get rid of the evidence, he disposed of the photos and his bloody clothes, then pushed the woman's car into the river.

Making his way back to his car, he sat for the longest time savoring his work. After the initial shock of what he'd done wore off, he felt an incredible high he had never experienced before. He felt empowered, alive. It wasn't until he had lain down for the night, did he realize the woman he killed resembled Lynette. He was angry because she didn't or wouldn't see what his brother was doing to her. From the first plunge of the knife to the last, he hated Lynette.

Bringing himself back to the present, Brody shook himself as if he'd caught a chill. He thought once Tony died the killing would stop, but it hadn't. It was too far gone for him to stop. Closing his eyes, he realized maybe he didn't want it to stop. He didn't want that sensation of power to end.

Dismissing the thought, Brody checked his watch. He had to leave now if he was to be on time for his meeting.

***

Kobe sat with KT in a booth at the diner where Brody wanted them to meet. It was two days before the election and they needed to execute their plan, if they were going to stop the voter fraud. They thought it was a no go after Tony was killed, but they discovered from their informant that the software's creator would be making the delivery directly. But at the moment that was the least of his worries. Each time there was a new body found in the river he felt he was missing something significant; something so important that it was eating away at him. He knew he should be concentrating on his job, but something wasn't right.

"Hey, you seem a million miles away. What's going on," KT asked him. She had noticed he was doing that a lot lately. Something was bothering him. She just hoped it wasn't Bria again, because it seemed he was getting pass his guilt.

Kobe shook his head to clear his thoughts. "Have you ever had a feeling that something was wrong? That there is something you're missing? Something is wrong KT and I just can't put my finger on it." That nagging feeling grew once Brody slid into the booth next to KT. She didn't get a chance to answer.

"Why so serious bro?" Brody asked of the scowl displayed on Kobe's face.

"Nothing, I'll just be glad when this is over, that's all." Kobe was beginning to wonder why he was uneasy around Brody. The man seemed likable enough.

KT watched Kobe shift gears. Whatever was bothering him, he didn't want Brody to know. She made a note to ask about it later. In her opinion, whatever Kobe was experiencing would come to light soon enough.

"Ok from what we've gathered, there is a warehouse down by the river where the software is being delivered. And from what my informant tells me the warehouse belongs to the mayor," Brody told them.

"Will the mayor be taking the delivery himself or will he be sending one of his flunkies to make the exchange?" Kobe asked.

"If I were him, I would be there myself; especially after Tony's death. I wouldn't want to be left out of the loop again. He and the chief thought all was lost because Tony was the only one who dealt with the guy, but they were given another opportunity. I'm sure he wouldn't want leave that up to chance a second time." KT knew she wouldn't.

Brody nodded. "We might get lucky and catch them both with their hands dirty. I would say the councilman would be there too, if his son wasn't still missing. The man is more concerned about him right now than keeping his seat."

KT checked her watch. They had just over an hour before the exchange was to take place. "Eric and his team will meet us there. Let's wrap this up tonight so the voters will be spared from these greedy bastards."

They all moved to head to the warehouse to take down the mayor and his crew. As Brody slid from the booth he shuddered. All of a sudden he felt drained. He was coming down off of his high. Unbeknownst to him, Kobe caught the change. Something was going on with Brody and he meant to find out what.

Chapter 25

KT ducked behind a column, narrowly avoiding the bullet that someone shot at her. She, Brody and Kobe, along with Eric and his men had cornered the crew in the warehouse. They had come to arrest the players in the voting machine fraud, only to stumble upon a much bigger operation.

As they quietly entered the massive building, they were surprised at what they saw. In one area of the common room, young women were cutting and packaging cocaine and heroin, while a group of men used counters to sort and count huge stashes of money on a nearby table. She and Kobe looked at each other as they witnessed the operation. They had no idea the voter fraud was just the tip of the iceberg.

As they waited for a signal from Eric, another group of women, all chained together, were led into the room from a door off to the side. The women were young, barely out of their teens. They were accompanied by a man and a woman, who KT recognized immediately. The woman was the salty bartender from the night she first met Kobe. She and Kobe looked at each other again. The man they recognized, was one of the crew from the bar that night.

"Why did you bring them in here?" This was from Riley Phillips. He was referring to the chained women. He had joined them from an office at the front of the building.

"Coburn wants to inspect his latest shipment," Teddy told him. He took the lead chain from Reese to lock it on a nearby steel bar, preventing any of the women from escaping.

Riley frowned. There was way too much activity going on today. He was just supposed to supply protection while Wallace and Hayes came down to meet with the software supplier, not to have Coburn thrown into the mix. He hoped Coburn would limit his inspection to just looking the girls over and not sampling the goods before he left. Riley's frown deepened. If it had been left up to him, he wouldn't have dealt with the girls at all, but that wasn't his call. He was just the overseer. It made him uneasy to watch the imprisoned and frighten women. He didn't know how or where Coburn acquired them and he didn't want to know. He didn't know why Wallace allowed the priest to become a part of their little family in the first place. He didn't trust the man. Besides, Coburn gave him the creeps.

"When are the bosses coming?" Another one of the men asked Riley.

"That's what I came out to tell you. They're not. They gave us the go ahead to handle this for them." Riley grinned. They were finally getting some respect. The bosses trusted them enough to handle something as important as the election. Maybe he wouldn't have to drop a dime on them after all. This thought brought another one; an unpleasant one. He still wished he could fish Ice out of his grave and kill him all over again.

"Hello boys." Brenda Sims strutted into the warehouse as if she owned the place. She grinned at the surprised expression on each of their faces.

"What the hell are you doing here?" Riley asked her. He recognized her from Grimes' office. She was Tony Grimes' assistant.

"I believe I have something that you want," she told the police sergeant. She found great joy in showing him the airhead had more brains than he gave her credit for.

Riley's eyes narrowed. It was no way this broad was who he was supposed to meet; no way. He watched, as she pulled a small package from her purse.

"And where is the mayor, I'm supposed to meet him and the councilman for the exchange." Brenda looked around the room. She wanted to see the look on that arrogant bastard's face, once he found out she was not only delivering the software, but also its author.

"They're not coming. You're dealing with me," Riley gladly informed her.

Brenda's smile immediately turned into rage. "That was not the deal! They were supposed to be here!." Brenda pointed toward the floor in front of her. She wanted both of their asses there, front and center.

Riley dismissed her attitude with a yawn. As long as he had her money why should she care if the bosses were there or not. "Do you want to do this or not. He pulled a thick package from his jacket pocket.

Brenda may have been angry, but she wasn't stupid. Shoving her package towards Riley, she grabbed his. Without another word, she turned on her heels to leave.

Riley inspected the contents. "Aren't you going to give us instructions on how to use it?" He asked the irate woman.

"It's in the bag." She never stopped walking.

Eric quietly radioed for her to be picked up the moment she cleared the door. He hoped the cops outside were able to whisk her out of sight before Coburn showed.

Riley shook his head grinning. He was still surprised at who had the software. All that time tearing up Grimes' office and house, and that bitch had it all along.

"Well that went better than expected." He tossed the package to Teddy. "Teddy, Reese, as soon as Coburn inspects his girls and leaves, I need for you two to deliver this to the mayor. He has some geek waiting to install it. And don't screw this up. If we do this right, we can handle more important stuff. You understand me?"

They both nodded. He would do it himself, but he wanted to make sure they got their shipment of drugs out on time. Not to mention there was another shipment of guns due in later that night. Hayes may have been distraught over his missing son, but he was still about his money flowing in.

When one of his men asked if they should move in, Eric motioned for everyone to hold their position. They had another player to add to the game—Father Coburn. He was

156 | P a g e

just as shocked as anyone when they heard the parish priest's name mentioned. He didn't know what to make of this. Father Mason Coburn running slavery and prostitution? Exactly what the hell had they stumbled into?

Chapter 26

Eric and his team watched the good Father inspect each of the chained women. The man fondled them and prodded them as if they were cattle. Motioning to his people, Eric silently instructed them to fan out. They were about to pull the plug on this unsavory mess.

After closely scrutinizing the last girl, Coburn pulled a notebook from his inner jacket pocket to jot down some notes. He nodded his approval. "These are perfect. Much better than the last crop. Make sure they get to their destination before midnight. I have a private party booked at 1:30 and they will be the entertainment. And make sure they're presentable. These men will only pay for the best quality, so pay attention to the smallest of details," he told Reese. He gave her a list of things he wanted implemented and the address to where the girls were to be taken for the private party.

After placing the notebook back into his pocket, he handed Reese her cut of the evening's profits. The moment the money exchanged hands, Eric gave the go ahead; flooding the poorly lit room with police officers. Once the building was teeming with police, the panicked occupants scattered throughout the warehouse; all except Mason Coburn. He was too stunned to move. Several of the criminals took a few shots at them before they were rounded up and cuffed. Father Coburn watched in disbelief, as he too was placed in restraints as the women he'd bought were unchained, and led out of the warehouse to safety.

Riley Phillips, hearing all the commotion from one of the offices, stuffed his pockets with money. "I have to get out of here." He peered through a crack in the wall watching as police rounded up the others. There was no way to escape through the front door. Searching the office for another route, he found some dilapidated boards along the back wall. Kicking out the rotted panels, he crawled outside only to be met by a gun to his face held by KT.

"Going somewhere?" She asked the fleeing man. Riley moved to stand to his feet. "Slowly now..." With the gun gripped in both hands, she kept it level with his head, as he slowly stood with his hands raised. She smiled when she saw recognition in his eyes.

All the color drained from Riley's face. The woman was a cop. Staring at her, he calculated what it would take to bring her down. He was completely sober this time, so there was no way she could get the best of him. He was still debating if he should take her on when Kobe grabbed him from behind, turning Riley to face him.

KT holstered her gun. "Didn't think I could handle it?" She asked Kobe. She'd notice he never left her side once they entered the warehouse.

Kobe shook his head. "Nah, I knew you had it. I just wanted to see the look on his face." He smiled as he placed the handcuffs on Riley. KT returned the smile. They both knew why he was there. He wanted to be close in case she needed saving.

Riley looked from one to the other. He couldn't believe it. The two were working together.

Chapter 27

Brenda Sims sat with her arms folded, staring at Detective Valero. She couldn't believe she had gotten caught. How could she have been so careless? She thought she had covered her tracks thoroughly, right up to the time the police grabbed her exiting the warehouse. They took her away so fast she didn't have a chance to protest.

"You ready to tell me how you got involved in all of this," Eric asked. They had been staring at each other for several minutes, without saying a word. He knew she was trying to decide if she should tell the whole truth or not. He had learned quite a bit about her since bringing her into the station.

Brenda Sims, better known as Sariah Leeks, was a software guru and hacker wanted by the FBI. She was one of the best computer specialists in the country, responsible for more than a dozen government security breaches. Moving from city to city, she changed her name to elude capture. Beyond that, he didn't know. He was curious to know how she became Tony Grimes' assistant.

Sighing, Sariah knew they had discovered who she was by now, so there wasn't any real reason not to talk. Besides, maybe she could negotiate this situation into something that would benefit her.

"Tony Grimes found out who I was and blackmailed me into helping him. I met him at a restaurant downtown. I thought it was a love connection, but it turned out to be a trap. He knew who I was all along and had been watching me for days; sizing me up. He came on quite charming and I thought he was a nice person until the blackmail." Sariah wrung her hands. It was time to explain the whole sorted mess.

Sariah had just settled into town when she met Tony. She had visited the diner many times for coffee while she searched through the want ads for a job. One morning he approached her and introduced himself. He noticed she was looking for employment and offered her a job. Everything was great at first. She loved the work, the pay was descent and she didn't mind the intimate lunches they shared. What better place to hide than right under everyone's nose in the assistant D. A.'s office.

She thought she was being clever, but Tony had plans for her. After the third time of meeting him for lunch in a nearby hotel room, she discovered she was trapped. Sariah learned that not only were they going to continue their 'lunch meetings', but she was going to help him become the next state representative.

There was nothing she could do. If she didn't cooperate, he would hand her over to the feds. So she reluctantly wrote the code for the software and continued their meetings. He promised he would let her leave after he sold the software to the mayor. But he was killed before he could make the exchange. She only continued with the trade, because she needed the money to leave the country.

Eric nodded. Tony Grimes was a bigger bastard than any of them knew. He wondered how many other women had he taken advantage of.

"You know," Sariah was saying. "I got great pleasure in letting his wife know he was cheating on her. When I heard she pulled a gun on him, I celebrated by getting drunk. I wished she had shot the bastard. But I guess everything still turned out right in the end." Sariah smiled then. When she heard Tony was dead she wanted to cry and scream in relief.

Eric frowned. So now there was a new suspect in Grimes' death. Although he still liked the wife for this murder, he couldn't be sure Sariah here wasn't the one who killed him.

"Did you kill him?"

Sariah shook her head. If I had killed him, it's no way I would have stuck around; payday or not. Besides, I had other ways of making his life a living hell. I could have ruined him in my world. And I had planned to do just that once I'd gotten far enough away from this place. I would have made damn sure he never stepped foot in the state capital."

Eric believed her. Having gathered all he needed from her, he prepared himself for his next interrogation— Mason Coburn.

Chapter 28

Mason Coburn sat on the metal chair with his head down and his eyes closed. Still wearing his collar, a casual observer would have thought he was praying. He was doing anything but. Father Mason Coburn was reminiscing. He was savoring his last encounter with his rare bird. So much so, he had an erection. When Eric stepped into the room, he had to call his name several times; snapping his fingers before his face, before he bothered to acknowledge him.

"Father, I know you were read your rights before you were removed from the warehouse, but I just want to make sure you understand them before our chat." Judging from his demeanor, Eric wondered if the man was even lucid.

Coburn nodded. "Yes detective, I understand. And I understand that you want some answers?" He raised a questioning brow at Eric.

"Yes I would. Like, how does a priest go from leading mass to dealing in prostitution?" Eric found him incredible. He seemed unfazed by his predicament.

Coburn shrugged. "It's quite simple detective. Why do people participate in anything these days…money?" Mason Coburn knew there was no way he was coming out of this completely clean, but he knew they didn't have much, not even with his laptop. But he also knew that was all they had.

He kept no records of his transactions with his overseas contacts or any of those he made with the mayor and his customers. The notebook they confiscated held only a few addresses and numbers that meant nothing unless he talked; and he had no plans to do so. The best they could do would be to charge him with what they witnessed today, and maybe try to make his accomplices' testimony stick. But what it came down to was their word against his. A good attorney could make most of what they had go away.

And as for the laptop itself, those were mostly videos of various men with various women with a few of him and his rare bird. It was just porn he acquired from various suppliers. The women in those videos were long gone and couldn't be used against him. And as for his bird, she would testify that she was a very willing participant. He had nothing more to say.

Chapter 29

Riley Phillips sat in the interrogation room cool as a cucumber. If he was going down, he sure as hell was taking the bosses with him. He learned, after he was arrested, the real reason Wallace and Hayes didn't show was because they were tipped off that the warehouse was going to be raided. They left him and his crew holding the bag. He knew they thought they were in the clear, but he had news for them. They would pay. He could just see Craven Wallace now, claiming he knew nothing about what was going on in his warehouse. And the rat bastard Allen will gladly back him up.

Riley grinned. Not only would he make sure those bastards paid, he would make sure the whole world knew Chief Allen's wife was a whore.

"What the hell…" Kobe couldn't believe what he was witnessing. Sergeant Riley Phillips sat in the interrogation room, as if he had the world by the tail and not on his way to prison. He shook his head. "Why is that asshole grinning like he knows something we don't?"

"I don't know, but I'm about to find out." Eric exited the room to visit with Phillips.

"Sergeant Phillips. You are in deep shit." He tossed a folder on the table outlining everything Phillips was being charged with. Eric didn't see how he could worm his way out of this mess.

"Do you want a lawyer, your union rep?" He was hoping he would decline both. He was anxious to put this mess to bed and concentrate on how to bring down Wallace, Hayes and Allen. He couldn't believe they might walk, if they couldn't come up with something concrete. Right now they only had rumors and hearsay situations. The men were smart. They never handled anything themselves; always keeping themselves several arms lengths away from their orchestrated crimes.

Riley shook his head. "I don't need them. But I do want to speak to the D.A. before we go any further." Riley grinned at Eric. "Oh and I would like my phone call please.

"Why do you want to see the D.A.?" Eric was beyond curious. Did he have something on Wallace and his cohorts?

"Just get him here. We'll all talk after my phone call." Riley watched Eric rise from his seat, take his folder and leave the room. Moments later one of his fellow officers entered to bring him a phone.

"What do you think that was all about?" KT asked Eric. She and Kobe were watching from the observation room.

Eric shook his head. "I don't know. But whatever it is, he seems pretty confident about it." Eric looked around the room. "Where is Brody? I thought he would want to be here for this. With all the people we've hauled in here, we may find his brother's killer amongst them." Even though he said this, Eric doubted it. His money was still on Lynette and if she did do it, he was pretty sure this crew knew nothing about it. There just wasn't any evidence to prove it.

"Detective, you might want to see this." An officer came into the room and plugged a flash drive into his laptop. "This is just one of the videos we found on Father Coburn's computer. I thought you might want to take a look at it."

As the group stood around the laptop, Lynette Grimes' image appeared on the screen; completely nude and being rode by Mason Coburn. Eric's brows lifted at this turn of events. Pausing the video, he noted the time and date stamp. It was right around the time Lynette's husband was being murdered.

"No wonder she didn't want to talk. She was with Coburn." KT shook her head in wonderment. Lynette Grimes had the nerve to hold a gun on her husband and his mistress, when she was having an affair of her own. She was getting it on with the priest.

"I wonder if she's one of his prostitutes or was she just having an affair." Kobe stated.

"Why don't we get her in here and ask her." Eric nodded at the officer who brought the video.

"Detective, turn on the TV." Another office stuck her head in the room. Picking up the remote control, Eric switched on the television. "It's on all of the news channels." Eric flipped the channels until he found what he was looking for.

"This just in…" The reporter gave them blow by blow accounts of the arrests they made that day. But what they weren't expecting was Sadie Allen's image to appear on the screen with an unknown man. Although the nude images were blurred out, it was pretty clear the couple were engaged in a sex act. The reporter went on to say that Police Chief Warren Allen's wife was part of a prostitution ring allegedly ran by parish priest Mason Coburn.

"From the look on Sadie's face, she wasn't a willing partner." KT commented.

"Just how many women did this asshole have under his thumb." Kobe couldn't believe it. He had come into this investigation with the hopes of stopping voter fraud, only to uncover much more.

"Officer, bring Coburn back into interrogation. Let's see if he has more to say now." He wanted to have another talk with the good Father.

"How did they get a hold of this footage? We're just now finding out about the videos ourselves." Eric asked. Then it dawned on him.

"Phillips!" He and KT came to the same conclusion. Eric flew from the room. He needed to talk to Phillips.

***

Riley Phillips was still grinning when Eric re-entered the room, this time with the D.A.

"Was that your doing…Sadie Allen?" he asked.

Riley grinned wider. "Now that I have your attention, I want to make a deal." He turned to the D.A.

"What do you have?" D.A. Garrett Pleasant asked Riley.

"You may not have proof that Mayor Wallace and Chief Allen were involved in the warehouse or the voter fraud, but I have proof they committed murder." Eric and Pleasant looks.

"Tell us what you know."

Chapter 30

Lynette Grimes was beside herself. "Oh God!" She was staring at the television screen. Mason had been arrested. She wondered what did that mean for her. Would Mason tell the police about their affair? She hadn't seen him since the night her husband was killed.

***

Lynette knew where she was headed the moment she left the house, but was uncertain if she should have come, once she was outside his door. She hadn't called first, which he insisted she do before coming to the rectory. Her hand shook as she raised it to tap on Father Coburn's door. She knew she shouldn't be there, but she couldn't help herself. She had to see him just one more time.

She sighed. Who was she fooling? She had told herself many times before that it would be the last time, but found herself standing outside his quarters anyway. Lynette rested her head against the cool wooden surface, wishing she could gather the courage to just walk away. She knew she could leave without any consequences, if she chose to. Mason didn't treat her as he did his other playmates. She was special to him; or so he said. Whenever any of his other women tried to leave, he used blackmail and violence to keep them in line. Although he never threatened her in any way, she often wondered if the unspoken threat of violence was what kept her coming back. As wonderful as he could be, she wouldn't put it past him to out and out destroy her.

***

Lynette thought of her mother. If her affair ever got out, it would kill her. Barbara always prided herself on how well she raised her children. Lynette wondered what she would think, if she knew how low her little girl had fallen. She was sleeping with a priest, for Christ's sake. Lynette tried to push Barbara Haymon out of her mind. Mama couldn't help her now. She was too far gone.

"Oh God, oh God…" Lynette bolted up from the sofa when the door bell rang.

Chapter 31

Brody Grimes was enraged. All this time he thought Lynette was innocent. All this time waiting to let his feelings be known to her, and she was having an affair of her own. She wasn't any better than his brother. In fact she was worse. The hypocritical bitch had the nerve to confront Tony on his cheating, when she was doing things far worse. Rolling around with that scum Coburn. He wondered how long had he been screwing her.

He had just cleared the doorway to the observation room when he saw Lynette on the computer screen with Coburn. At first he thought maybe she was being coerced into having sex with the priest, but soon recognized she was a willing participant. He backed out of the room before the others knew he was there. Breaking speeding laws to get to Lynette's house, he wanted answers.

Brody clenched and unclenched his fists, as he waited for her to answer the door. This bitch was going to pay and pay dearly. Sweeping past her when she finally opened the door, he waited for her in the living room. Before she could ask why he was there, he slapped her.

"You bitch…how could you do those vile things with that…that fraud?"

Lynette's eyes widened. *He knows! Oh my God he knows!* She backed away from him; trying to put some distance between them. Her head was spinning more from the revelation that he knew than from the attack.

Brody took a step towards her. "Brody wait…" Lynette held out her hands as she moved farther from him. She didn't want him to hit her again. "Please just calm down."

"How could you give yourself to another man? How could you? I was always here…me…right here!" he pointed at himself.

It finally dawned on Lynette why he was so upset. He wanted her for himself. She thought he was angry because of his brother. But now she knew better.

"I waited for you Lynette. I waited for you to see Tony for what he was and come to me. I loved you…I would have taken care of you." Brody was walking around in circles now. He was talking more to himself than he was Lynette. "I loved you…Tony didn't love you, I loved you! You have no idea what I've done for you! No idea at all."

He whispered this last sentence. Focusing back on Lynette he moved towards her, swiftly grabbing her by her hair. "I want some of what you gave Coburn and you're going to give it to me."

Dragging her into her bedroom, Brody threw her on the bed. "Take off your clothes." When she didn't move fast enough, he pulled his knife from the sheath attached to his belt. "Now!"

Lynette slowly began to unbutton her blouse. What was she going to do? Brody was out of his mind. She had to think. She remembered her gun only to further remember Brody had taken it away from her, after she held Tony and Cassie with it. She had gotten to the last button when the doorbell rang. She screamed out, before Brody hit her in the mouth, knocking her backwards onto the bed. The officers outside heard the outcry and started beating on the door. With no answer they broke it down. When they reached Lynette, Brody was gone. He had left through the patio doors.

***

"Detective, there has been an incident at the Grimes' house.

Eric and Pleasant had just finished taking Phillips statement. Two detectives were on their way to retrieve the video of Wallace and Allen committing murder. Phillips had explained how he had come about the evidence, leaving out the part of killing Ice and the photos of Nadia. He told them he found the evidence provided by an anonymous tip. He explained that a friend had emailed the video of the Chief's wife to all the news outlets at his request. It was the phone call he'd made. The other evidence was in a safe deposit box at his bank.

If the evidence panned out, he would be spending minimum of two years jail time in a low security facility in protective custody.

"What's the problem?"

"Mrs. Grimes was attacked by her brother in law."

"What?" The officer explained the circumstances surrounding Lynette's attack.

"What the hell is going on? He attacked her with a knife? Put an all points out for him."

Suddenly, Kobe realized what had been bothering him—Brody's knife. The first time he saw it was at

Lynette's after Brody talked her into coming out of the bedroom. He had joined him just before Lynette stepped into the hallway. Brody was placing the knife back into its sheath. He remembered noting that it had an oddly shaped blade with a jagged edge just on the tip. In light of what happened that day, he had forgotten about it. But if he was right, Brody may be responsible for all the bodies dumped in the river.

"We need to find him..Now!"

Chapter 32

Warren Allen sat in Craven Wallace's office horrified. They had been waiting for the delivery of the voter machine software, when the breaking news came across the television screen. Not only had their little enterprise been busted by his own men, but his wife was one of Coburn's whores. He wanted to kill the man.

Pointing his finger at Craven, Warren leaped from his chair. "This is your goddamn fault. I told you that damn priest wasn't to be trusted. This bastard couldn't just stick to the women we smuggled, nooo… he had to involve my wife. I bet that sick prick laughed many a night at what he'd done. And did you recognize the man with her? Hayes is going to blow a gasket." The man in the video with Sadie Allen was Councilman Hayes' father in law. Warren couldn't believe it. That old bastard was plugging his wife.

As if on cue, Big Ed let himself into the mayor's office. "Did you see this shit?" He screamed. He was pointing at the now muted television screen. "How the hell did my father in- law get involved in this shit?"

Big Ed pointed at Warren. "And you...You couldn't control your fucking wife?" Warren lunged at the councilman, grabbing him by the collar, before Craven could come between them.

"Stop it! We have bigger worries right now." He let go of the two men. "Is there anything that can lead the police back to us...anything?" He felt there wasn't, but with the way their luck was running, he wouldn't bank on it.

"You personally made a deal for the software," Hayes reminded him, straightening his rumpled tie.

"If that little bitch knows what's good for her, she will keep her mouth shut. Besides, it's her word against mine. She can't prove a thing. She was paid in cash, so..." Craven hoped it would be enough to keep them out of jail. As for Coburn, he didn't have to worry about him. All of their transactions were done through Phillips.

And speaking of Coburn, he almost laughed out loud thinking how Warren went off. He didn't know the half of it. He was responsible for Sadie being caught up with Coburn. He had always wanted Sadie, ever since their street days. So when they all came up out of the gutter together, he thought he had a chance. He knew she wasn't happy with her husband. He was always working, never paying her much attention. But when he made a play for her, she turned him down. Saying he was still the same old gutter scum dressed up in tailored suits. She always blamed him for getting her husband involved in the street life. She wanted Warren to go to college and make something good out of himself.

The snotty bitch wouldn't even give him credit for the lifestyle they now had. If it hadn't been for him, her husband would still be working the streets or dead. When he discovered she had a thing for Coburn, he made a deal with him to turn her out. He fixed that bitch good; they were even now. She would always be known as Metro City's number one whore. And one day he would let her know he was the one who put her there.

Shifting his attention, Craven picked up a decanter of expensive whiskey to pour himself a shot. He needed it to bring some calm to the situation. If everyone kept their heads, they could walk away from this thing without ending up in prison. He may not be able to ensure another term as mayor, but at least he would be free. Besides, they had made more than enough money to last them several lifetimes. They should count this as a blessing and not as a problem. It was time to call it quits. Now all he had to do was get Ed and Warren on board.

Chapter 33

"We have to find him…we have to find him now!" Kobe was pacing, trying to think. He couldn't believe he missed it.

"Kobe, what's wrong?" KT was worried. She hadn't ever seen him this agitated.

He stopped pacing to turn to KT. "What do you know about that knife he carries?"

KT shrugged. "I think it's from his days in the marines. He's had it as long as I've known him. What about it?"

Instead of answering her, Kobe turned to Eric. "Eric. The knife that was used to kill those women, it was oddly shaped with a serrated tip, right?"

Eric slowly nodded; trying to pick up where he was going with this. "Yeah…"

"Brody's knife fits that description," Kobe pressed.

"You can't believe he had anything to do with those killings." KT was in disbelief.

184| P a g e

"Did you think he would have attacked Lynette?" he asked her; further driving his position.

She didn't have an answer for that. He had a point. And what was that all about anyway? Why would he attack Lynette? He loved her. *He loved her. He loved her!*

KT's eyes widened. "Oh my God…he loves her! Maybe he found out about her and Coburn…but Kobe, that doesn't mean he killed those women." She was still trying to give Brody the benefit of the doubt. She just couldn't see it.

Kobe turned to Eric. "You're quiet. What are you thinking?" He needed one of them to see the light and quickly.

Eric shook his head. "I don't know what to think. But when we find him, we will get to the bottom of this."

***

Brody was going crazy. He didn't mean to lose control like that, but Lynette made him so angry. He paced up and down the dock trying to clear his head and decide on what to do next. He had to think. There was only one thing that usually calmed him down, and the opportunity was tied up in the trunk of his car. If he was going to get out of this mess, he had to do this one last kill. They had no evidence that he was the killer they were looking for, and he could easily explain away his anger at Lynette. He was just upset after learning of her affair with Coburn. After all, she was married to his brother.

His brother. He laughed out loud. Had he known what a whore Lynette was, he never would have killed him. Everything he did that night was for Lynette. She was so upset when she left the house. All that bastard had to do was let her go. But no…he couldn't do that. He had to stick around to make her life more unbearable.

He knew exactly where Tony was headed that night, over to that whore Cassie's. He never stopped sleeping with the dumb bitch. Didn't she know he was screwing his assistant? Brody shook his head with remembrance. He had made the mistake of coming to Tony's office unannounced, to find him there with Brenda bent over his desk. The bastard didn't have the decency to stop what he was doing when he walked in on them. He just kept right on going; laughing as he left.

Brody thought about killing Cassie but he needed her. After he left Tony's office, he sat outside of her apartment and waited until she left then let himself inside. Finding what he needed, he took the note she'd left and sat in his car, until his brother arrived. He hit him over the head while he admired himself in the mirror, dragging him across the parking lot to his trunk.

Brody drove him to the secluded dock where he and Tony fished as kids with their father. When Tony came to, he confronted him about Lynette. Tony just laughed at him, saying how he knew he had a stiff one for his wife. The bastard told him he could have her. He was about finished with her anyway. When Tony turned his back, Brody took the knife he'd taken from Cassie's apartment and stabbed him. He kept stabbing him until he stopped moving, and then pushed his body into the river.

He thought once Tony was gone Lynette would come to him, but she didn't. Now he knew why. She was screwing Coburn.

It was time he soothed his frustrations. He may not be able to get to Lynette, but he could make himself happy just the same. Turning on his heels, Brody stalked back up the wooden dock to his car. Hitting the key fob he popped open the trunk. A gagged and bound Cassie Duvall peered up at him.

Chapter 34

Lynette hugged herself while she waited for someone to come in to talk to her. She had been placed in an office alone after arriving at the police station. She could tell her secret was out the moment she was escorted into the building. Everyone stopped what they were doing to gaze at her. Everyone now knew she was sleeping with Mason.

Rubbing her arms as if she were cold, she let her mind drift back to the day she met Mason Coburn. Sadie Allen had asked for her help in teaching her literacy class that night. She was down with the flu, but didn't want to disappoint her students since they were making such great progress.

She had just finished the class when Mason entered the room. He introduced himself and helped her clean up. As they talked, they learned they had a lot in common. They were from the same home town and knew some of the same people. Lynette found him charming and attentive; unlike her husband who had become unavailable emotionally and physically, since deciding to run for state office. The long nights that kept him late at the office, had become nights he didn't bother to come home at all; always with the excuse he fell asleep working on his campaign. She now knew he was working on Cassie and God only knew who else.

When Mason suggested they have dinner, she accepted. One dinner turned into two and two turned into a heated affair. They were having dinner at the rectory when he kissed her for the first time. She was put off at first, because of her marriage and his standing in the church. But Mason made it difficult to resist the temptation to be held and loved again. He was gentle and loving in bed. Making her feel like the most special woman on earth and she enjoyed every moment of his attention.

Lynette placed her face in her hands. She never meant for it to last as long as it did. It was suppose to be a onetime thing, but Mason's demeanor was so intoxicating, making it hard to say no. She knew she should have put a stop to it, long before she found out about the other women; one being Sadie Allen.

She was devastated when she discovered she wasn't the only woman in Mason's life. After watching Sadie hurry from his room one night, she confronted him. She was surprised when he made no attempts to lie or explain away Sadie's visit. He made no excuses for his actions and left it at that. She shook her head as she remembered how she stormed out, vowing never to return again. But she had returned, and many more times after that.

Lynette sat up when the door opened, bringing Detective Valero and another man inside. She remembered him being one of the people at her home when she caught Tony cheating. The detective settled in the chair across from her, While Kobe stood near the door.

"Mrs. Grimes, Lynette. Before we get to why your brother in-law attacked you, do you have any idea where he may have gone?" Eric studied her. If Kobe was right, they needed to find him fast.

Lynette shook her head. She was still trying to piece together how she could have missed Brody's feelings for her. She loved her brother-in law but not in that way. He was Tony's brother.

"Think…any place you can think of that may be a special or private place for him. Some where he may go to clear his head." Eric knew he was pushing, but if Brody was their serial killer, Lynette's affair may have sent him over the edge enough to kill again.

Lynette tapped the desktop in remembrance. "Yes!…there's a place along the river that he and Tony used to talk about. It's a secluded cabin or shack or something on his family's property. Their father used to take them fishing there when they were kids. Tony took me there once, but I don't think he spent much time there as an adult. The place didn't hold the same memories for him as it did for Brody. But I do remember Brody mentioning that he goes there from time to time. I think he still maintains the place for hunting season.

Pulling a map from a shelf behind him, Eric spread it out across his desk. Kobe moved to stand behind Lynette. "Can you show us where this place is located?"

Lynette shrugged. "I guess I could. After showing them the location of the property, Kobe, Eric and KT left to look for Brody.

Chapter 35

Cassie's wide eyes followed Brody as he paced the dock, ranting about Lynette. He had taken her from the trunk and carried her down to the end of the pier. She tried to remember what happened. She remembered coming out of her apartment to get in her car, and that was the last thing she could recall until waking up in darkness. The last person she expected to see when the trunk opened was Tony's brother Brody. She didn't understand why she was there or why he'd taken her.

Cassie flinched when Body turned and kicked at her. The more he raged, the more she shook with fear. When he turned to curse at the river, she took this chance to take in her surroundings; hoping there was someone near to help her. That hope soon deflated. There wasn't anything or anyone in sight. All she saw was miles and miles of woods and brush. She had no idea where she was. As she looked down on where she was sitting, she realized she was planted in the middle of a big pool of dried blood. Her eyes and fear grew even wider.

Brody stopped pacing to look at her. "I knew Tony was cheating with you. I wanted him to fall in love and leave Lynette…and…and just go off somewhere, anywhere with you. But my brother never loved anyone but himself. Did you know he was screwing his assistant while he was screwing you?" Brody laughed. "You side bitches always think you're the only ones."

Taking his knife from his belt, he squatted beside Cassie. "I just knew it was over once Lynette found out about you…woo whoo…and when she caught you together…man that was a high! I almost wished she had killed Tony, and then I wouldn't have had to."

Cassie stopped breathing. He killed Tony. Brody's face had become an unrecognizable twisted mask of its former self. She thought she would faint. All this time she believed Lynette had finished what she'd started that day in her bedroom. Brody was insane.

Standing again he continued. "And it would have been over, if that selfish bastard had just left Lynette alone. He wanted to stay in the same house with her until after the election. Can you believe that? He gets caught cheating and had the nerve to still make demands." Brody started pacing again, twirling the knife, making circles in the air with it.

"I couldn't let that happen. He had hurt Lynette enough. It was time he left and left for good. It was my time with her." Brody grinned then.

"Do you know what I did?" he asked Cassie. "I waited until you left that night and let myself into your house. I borrowed one of your biggest and sharpest knives and I waited for my dear brother to show up. I knew he would make his way to your place after he topped off his assistant. I called him to make sure he would be there. When he stepped out of his car I knocked him unconscious and brought him right here." He pointed with his knife to the spot Cassie was sitting on.

"I waited for him to come around and I confronted him about Lynette. The bastard just laughed. He told me I could have her once he was done with her and not a moment before. He said he knew all about my little crush on his wife and thought it was pathetic. That I should have been man enough to take what I wanted, instead of waiting around like some weak ass punk. He laughed so hard that he was doubled over. That's when I took your knife and I stabbed his ass until I got tired. I pushed him into the river and as they always say, the rest is history." Brody took a bow as if he were performing a part in a play.

"I wanted to kill two birds with one stone that night. Kill him and frame you for it. You were the scorned ex-lover who was angry her man stayed with his wife. But you lucked out my dear. Someone saw you that night, so I couldn't pin it on you. Just my luck." He snapped his fingers. So instead of placing the knife where the cops could find it, I just tossed it. It had served its purpose."

"But when the cops couldn't pin you for it, they went after Lynette. Man…I almost had a melt down on that one. I did everything to steer them away from her and they landed on her anyway; all because she didn't have an alibi…or so we all thought at the time." Brody was agitated again thinking of Lynette with Coburn.

"Who knew that bitch was a bigger whore than my brother. Yeah, she had an alibi alright. She was sleeping with a priest! Can you believe that? After all I'd done to be with that bitch she was spreading 'em for a priest for god's sake!" He laughed maniacally.

"You know what…enough talking, I need to feel better and the only way to do that is for me to kill you sweetie pie." With the gag muffling her sobs, Cassie started to cry. "Ah, sweet girl. Don't cry; it's nothing personal. You just happened to be handy that's all. I'd planned to kill

Lynette's ass, but the cops showed up. And I didn't have time to coddle and prime someone else. That would have taken way too much time. I need to feel better about all of this…Lynette and that priest! I need to feel better now!" Picking Cassie up by an arm, he placed the blade against her cheek.

"Put the knife down Brody, it's over!"

Chapter 36

Bouncing her left leg, Reese Phillips glanced around the dingy gray room. She was scared. She had always looked to her brother Riley to keep her out of jail, him being the police and all. But this time he couldn't. He was about to do some prison time himself. If it hadn't been for the mayor and his scheme to get re-elected, the cops still wouldn't have known about their activities.

She shook her head. Why couldn't they have had their little exchange somewhere else? And to top it all off, it looked like Wallace and Allen would get away scot free. There was nothing concrete tying them back to the warehouse. They had their flunkies to pin it on, including her and her brother. Maybe she had enough information on some of the others to make a deal. Reese finally had hope.

"Miss Teresa Phillips." Detective Valero had joined her in the interrogation room. Even though he was still reeling from Brody's confession to killing his brother, plus evidence tying him to the multiple murders, he still had work to do. He took the chair opposite of Reese; tossing a baggy containing evidence on the table.

Reese recognized the item in the small plastic bag. It was her charm bracelet. She wondered what her bracelet had to do with anything. Reese stared at it as Eric removed it from the baggy. It was one of her prized possessions. Teddy had given it to her on her birthday. She knew Teddy was sweet on her, but at the time, all she wanted was Carrington Hayes. Reese frowned. Carrington didn't even bother to recognize her birthday let along give her a gift. Her face softened. She should have been nicer to Teddy.

Eric held the bracelet up to the light. "Nice bracelet." And he meant it. It wasn't cheap either. Reese was literally wearing thousands of dollars on her wrist. Made of white gold, each charm, thirteen in all, was embedded with high quality diamonds.

"There are what? Thirteen charms here?" he shifted his focus from the bracelet to Reese.

Reese shook her head. "No, fourteen…there are fourteen charms. Teddy placed exactly fourteen charms on that bracelet. He said he added the extra one for luck. He said thirteen of anything was bad luck." Reese smiled at this memory. Yes, she should have been nicer to Teddy. He deserved it. It was a beautiful bracelet, but she had accepted it as if he had handed her a piece of paper. She couldn't let him know how much she liked it. She didn't want to give him the wrong impression.

"Well I guess Teddy was correct. Thirteen is a bad number for you. One of the charms is missing from this bracelet." He turned it around so she could see the empty space. "But don't worry though, we found it. It was in the cuff of one of Carrington Hayes' pant legs."

Reese's hands flew to her mouth with a gasp. They found Carrington's body.

After learning of Brody's escapades, they dragged along the banks of the river near, Brody's killing ground and the raided warehouse. After coming across another one of Brody Grimes' victims, entangled in a fishing net, the divers discovered the barrel containing Carrington's body.

"I didn't mean to kill him…you got to understand I didn't mean too…" Reese was in a panic. Teddy swore to her Carrington would never be found. After that day, she just put Carrington's death out of her mind, never to be thought of again. She never expected him to be found.

"Listen…I have information on the mayor and his sidekick Allen. I can help you get them!" Reese was desperate. She had to find a way to get out of this mess.

Eric shook his head. "Your brother and boyfriend have beaten you to the punch on that one. They provided evidence that will put both of them away for a long time.

After viewing the video of their mayor and police chief executing a known drug dealer, other tidbits of information was provided by another source. There was someone else who had a few videos of his own—Teddy Reid.

Teddy claimed he needed some insurance policies in case the bosses ever got the idea to turn on them. He got the idea after Riley refused to tell the bosses about Ice's evidence, which in turn placed Riley Phillips in the hot seat for Ice's murder. Teddy also tied Councilman Hayes to the prostitution and drug ring, netting the department a pretty good day in arrests.

Epilogue

"Not a bad day's work. We managed to stop the election fraud and capture some criminals we had no idea we were looking for," Eric told the group. He, KT, Kobe and Tor were having drinks in the bar where it all started.

"Why? I mean, why did Brody do it?" This was KT. She had worked with Brody for a number of years and had no idea what he was capable of. She had hoped Kobe was wrong about him, right up to his confession that he killed his brother. She just couldn't understand it.

Once they arrived at the shack, they were able to overhear his confession of killing Tony and his plans for Lynette. After he was confronted on the pier, he shoved Cassie into the water, bound and unable to swim. They had to scramble to keep her from drowning. Kobe was the one who saved her. And as for his other crimes, after he was arrested, the knife he used was linked to the killings.

"The surprise for me was Coburn. Did he explain how he became a part of the mayor's crew?" Kobe wasn't the only one who was surprised. That pretty much was the sentiment from the entire group.

Eric shook his head. "Although he has yet to admit to any wrong doings, I honestly believe he tried to clean up the neighborhood and actually thought he had made a difference with Wallace and Allen. But instead of cleaning up the streets, as they promised, they just flooded it with more crimes. He may have given over to the attitude, if you can't beat 'em…" Eric shrugged; not needing to finish the cliché.

"But human trafficking and prostitution? He was a man of the cloth." Tor couldn't understand how Coburn, being a priest, could have participated in such a heinous crime. If he had a choice, he would have preferred the man was caught dealing drugs.

"Where Wallace and Allen's downfall was power, Coburn's was women. And because we have a weak case against him, he may walk. Any of the women who could testify against him are long gone. Sadie Allen is too ashamed to get involved, not to mention her involvement started with an affair with him, which quickly turned into blackmail." Eric wasn't happy about any of this.

"Let's not forget Lynette Grimes was a willing participant," Tor added. "She has nothing to testify to other than her own infidelity.

KT shook her head. "For me it's not just the women, but the power and control he had over them. According to Sadie Allen, Coburn is a cruel and evil man. He got off on hurting and manipulating her. All of the johns he chose for her were just as sadistic as he is."

"From watching those videos, some of them were pretty sick. If I could have foretold anyone committing murder, it would have been Sadie killing Coburn. Not only did he set her up with those assholes, he made her visit him before each of her encounters with these men." Eric wished he could lock the bastard up and throw away the key.

With her husband in jail, and all of their assets frozen, he wondered how Sadie would get by. After the scandal broke, she couldn't even go back to teaching, if she wanted to. No school district would hire an alleged ex-prostitute, coerced or not.

"What do you make of Coburn's and Lynette's relationship?" Kobe asked.

"Personally, I think he had feelings for Lynette. She was the only one of the women whom he didn't have tricking for him," Eric told him.

"And those videos seem to support this." KT added. "She was only seen in ones with him, no one else. I guess it was just bad judgment on her part."

KT asked Lynette about Coburn. She said it was as if she were addicted to him. She couldn't stay away even though there was always the chance someone would find out. She was also asked why she continued to let Tony live at the house after she caught him cheating. That's when she told them about the bank accounts. It was discovered Tony had lied about having one in her name. He only used the ruse to keep her in line. Lynette had been relieved. A part from their joint accounts, financially Lynette would be ok. Unlike Sadie Allen whose money was tied to her husband's.

Eric tilted his beer bottle to his lips. Yes, it had been a good day.

***

Kicking off his shoes Kobe settled deeper into his sofa. It had been a long two weeks, but he had survived them. And the best part, no one got hurt. He found joy from this. All during the investigation he had little sleep and little time to think about Bria. Was he losing her or was he finally letting go of the guilt. He decided it was the latter. Like KT said, he could never forget her. She would always be a part of him; always be his heart.

As for KT, he had to check himself when it came to his temporary partner. The more time he spent with her, the more he liked her. In fact, he began to like her a little too much. This wouldn't have been a problem had he not valued Eric Valero's friendship. Never one to venture into another man's territory, there was no way he was going to start with KT. Besides, he could plainly see she was in love with Eric.

Turning on the television, Kobe queued the football game he'd recorded earlier. It was late, but he didn't have to go into the office for another couple of days. Settling himself more comfortably on the couch, Kobe laid his head back. But instead of watching the game, for the first time in a year, he had fallen into a sound and peaceful sleep.

www.ingramcontent.com/pod-product-compliance
Lightning Source LLC
Chambersburg PA
CBHW030322180626
46810CB00003B/1197